5-Minute Bedtime Stories
for Kids

Bedtime Stories that will Make Kids and
Adults Laugh. A Book for Children with a
Very Special Moral Lesson

Clara Farrell

Table of Contents

the publisher or the original author of this work can be in any fashion deemed liable for any hardship or damages that may befall them after undertaking information described herein.

Additionally, the information in the following pages is intended only for informational purposes and should thus be thought of as universal. As befitting its nature, it is presented without assurance regarding its prolonged validity or interim quality. Trademarks that are mentioned are done without written consent and can in no way be considered an endorsement from the trademark holder.

Introduction

Reading is the most important thing we can teach our children, reading is as essential today as breathing. Children will not be able to survive nowadays if they don't know how to read. We all know that learning and education begins at home. Parents should try to teach their kids how to read as soon as possible to provide them an edge when its time for them to go to school.

One way of encouraging kids to read is to read to them, the bedtime stories our parents use to read to us are not only to entertain us before we go to sleep but to also encourage us to learn how to read. Research shows that kids who read to by their parents when they were young are better at reading and studying.

Now as parents are duty is to provide reading materials to our kids that are tailored made for them. Reading materials that will encourage our kids not just to read, but learn about new things and acquire extra knowledge like about animals and their natural habitats. There are a lot of materials out there we can give our kids to encourage them to read. There are books, games, toys and many more that we can give them. But as we know, kids today have a very short attention span, if the thing we provide them does not interest them or intimidate them they will not even spend five minutes with it. Books are a good source of material that we can give to our kids, but most of the time kids find books intimidating and really boring because of the lack of visual materials. Kids learn better and faster if they have visual stimulation.

The art of telling a good bedtime story dates back quite far. This remarkable discovery speaks volumes as to the importance of telling bedtime stories to your child. Parents for literally thousands of years have told variations of the stories told today. It is an oral tradition of great importance and one that all parents should be doing. Not only is a bedtime story fun and relaxing, it is also an effective and important way to become closer with your child.

What Is a Bedtime Story?

Bedtime stories are stories that are told after your child has gotten into bed for the evening. Many times they will ask for you to sit with them. This is an easy opportunity to offer to tell them a story. Young children especially love this because it is a treat for them and makes them feel truly important at that moment.

You can either read a classic story from a book, find a quick one online, or tell one from memory. Oftentimes a great bedtime story is improvised to suit the mood of your child in that particular moment. These stories are typically ones that have been told for many years in many different ways. Popular stories include ones about princesses and princes, great monsters and knights, children on adventures, and exciting tales with no particular ending to them. This latter type of story is interesting because it allows you to draw the same story out over many nights to keep your child interested and always wanting more.

Develop Memories Together

Reading a bedtime story to your children is a great way to connect with them. It brings the family closer in an intimate setting that also makes the child feel special. Memories are made as stories are told. Your child will look forward to you sitting with them before they drift off to sleep. This time together is something that they will always cherish. These precious moments benefit everyone involved, and you will find that you look forward to the bedtime stories almost as much, or more than your little one.

Benefits Of Bedtime Stories

Telling bedtime stories is beneficial. Your child will find sleep coming in a peaceful way with a great story in their ears. It engages their imagination while giving them good dream material, and has been shown to calm down a busy child. Children do tend to be worked up at times, especially at night, and a nice story will put their fears to rest and allow them much-needed relaxation. You can make a story that shows them that the monster under their bed is not so bad, or that the shadows on their wall are their friends. The possibilities are endless with creative solutions to any nighttime issue.

Bedtime stories also teach your child in ways that are similar to fables, myths, and fairy tales. Reading bedtime stories is a compelling way of helping your child grow into a well-shaped individual. The fun part about bedtime stories is that you can make one up yourself and craft it into something unique and special. A special story goes a long way for a child with open ears, and you will become a source of great interest to your children.

How The Unicorn Got Its Horn

The last short story I found in my notebook that I want to share with the world. Enjoy!

Once upon a time, there lived a beautiful caramel-colored horse. It had a long, flowing mane and polished hooves. He was the envy of all the horses.

One day, a woman was bleaching her gowns in a large pot, outside in the fresh air. Now, the horse was enjoying himself and having fun in the breeze, and accidently landed in the pot after a soaring jump.

His skin, mane, and hooves were completely white.

"Oh, no," he thought. "Now I am ust a common horse!"

He ran off in grief, deep into the woods. And he hid. Days went by and eventually a man learned of his disappearance. He held a sack of horns, bleached white, collected from horned animals. Upon hearing the man approach, the horse slowly moved out from behind the emerald green bushes to show himself.

The man was holding horns to sell, but of course nobody wanted horns for anyting. Interested, the horse grabbed a horn from the sack and played with it, and the man shrugged. He left quickly and the horse let him.

He soon came upon a reflective river, and looked at his appearance. He decided to play dress-up, a s he was bored, and put sticky sap at the end of his horn, and put it on his forehead.

He laughed and tried to pull it of. Unfortunately, it wouldn't come off, and he had to go on with the horn. He pranced through the villiage and people stared, but he proudly galloped on.

He eventually met a wonderful wife, and they had many children. Each of them had a horn. Eventually, unicorns became a real animal, but they had to run away and hide, since every person wanted to capture one for a pet.

The story spread that the race of the unicorns died, and nobody speaks of unicorns now. But one day, deep in the woods, if you look carefully, you just might see a unicorn, prancing amongst the trees.

The Legend Of The Unicorn

Once upon a time in a kingdom far-far-away in the lands of the never-ending spring, a king sat in his golden throne and ruled his kingdom in perfect harmony. A person can feel nothing but exuberance at the sight of the magnificent castle in which the king and his daughter lived, the majestic atmosphere of the woods spread all around the castle, and last but not least the overwhelming beauty of the princess. It was pure Heaven-on-Earth; there was nothing that could even possibly attain the perfection of this place. The beauty of the forest made it amazing, yet another thing made it imposing. In those woods lived creatures of time unknown and one of them was the most precious of them all... and was hunted for centuries for its magical horn the beast known as a unicorn.

One day a rumor started spreading. Someone saw a white creature with the looks of a horse, yet having a beautiful horn... and suddenly all men grabbed their knives and spears, their bloodlust and fierceness. The hunt had begun. While the king's men were all setting torches on fire and sharpening their tools, the young princess was at her chamber, brushing her beautiful silky blond hair. She was the purest maiden in the whole kingdom with a heart as tender as a rose and a soul as clean as the water from the Fountain of Youth in the woods. She had an adventurous spirit and that day she decided to take a walk in the surrounding forests. Pushed by the desire to pick some fresh flowers, she left the castle and headed towards the woods.

With all beauty of the trees and flowers and the crystal cleanness of the mineral springs she lost track of time and wandered around for hours and hours and suddenly, she was very deep into the woods.

She started realizing that the woods were getting darker and darker and the trees were losing their beauty, the grass was dead and there were no animals around. She started getting scared and remembered a story heard long ago from her nanny, a story about the Dark Forest, deep inside the beautiful surrounding woods. Everyone believed it was just a legend, that it wasn't a real place, but right at that moment she was thinking it over. "Could it be tr..." she couldn't even finish her thought when tree branches started grabbing her legs and arms and taking her deeper and deeper into the forest...

The creature was stepping lightly onto the grass, slowly moving between the trees, heading towards the little glade where she was lying unconsciously. As approaching, it saw the purity of the girl in front of him and slowly began to trust that innocent maid.

When the unicorn got to her, he bent his neck down and looked at her beautiful face and slowly lied down next to her. After a while she woke up and firstly got a little scared, yet after looking at its harmless black eyes, she felt safe. Then the white beast stood up and let her get on its back and they both headed towards the castle. The princess was charmed by that creature's innocence and nobility, by its graceful movements between the trees and its gentle steps on the grass pure harmony.

When they reached the castle and went inside the stone walls all of a sudden, a lot of armed people surrounded them and the unicorn started neighing and moving abruptly. The princess got down on the ground and started screaming and telling the men that this creature saved her life and brought her back to the castle. When the king came, she explained him everything that happened and he, while crying, told her that everyone had gotten worried about her. He hugged his precious daughter and looked at the terrified beast. Not until then he did realize that the unicorn is the purest and the most innocent creatures of them all.

During the feast that night, it was pronounced that the unicorn is a sacred animal and it was forbidden hunting it.

After saving the young princess, the beast left the castle and never got back. No one ever saw it again, but now all men knew the truth about the unicorn. It is said that the king's daughter met the unicorn again....

The Unicorn and The Pegasus

The unicorn had been very jealous of her flying friend, the Pegasus; a winged white stallion that could swoop and soar and loop the loop through the air.

"I wish that I had wings upon my back and could fly up to the wide, blue sky like that", the unicorn always thought, whenever she saw the Pegasus flying.

Then, one day, a balloon salesman came to the magic meadow where the Pegasus and the unicorn lived and he had a big bunch of brightly coloured, helium filled balloons on strings.

Seeing all the balloons gave the Unicorn a wonderful idea and, giving the balloon seller one of her golden horse shoes, the unicorn bought the biggest one that the balloon seller had and she tied the string at the end of it round the middle of her body.

Then, all of a sudden, the unicorn saw her hooves start to rise off of the ground and before long the unicorn was floating high in the air, suspended from the large, lighter than air balloon.

"Look! Look!", called the unicorn to the Pegasus who was hovering nearby, "I'm flying! I'm flying!".

But the Pegasus just shook his head and tutted, "If unicorns were meant to fly then Mother Nature would have given them wings like mine", he said.

This only irritated the unicorn who refused to listen and instead turned up her nose haughtily.

But, just then, the unicorn heard a loud popping sound from above her head, "Oh dear!", she said, looking up, "My horn has burst the balloon!".

Then, suddenly, the unicorn started to fall very fast towards the ground. "Oh no!", she cried in panic, "Help! Help! I'm falling!".

Fortunately, the Pegasus saw the falling unicorn and swooped down to help his friend, catching the unicorn between his hooves and flying it safely to the ground.

"I told you", said the Pegasus, "Unicorns just aren't meant to fly".

But then the Pegasus felt a sudden, terrible sharp pain in his left wing and, looking back, he saw that he had broken it.

"Oh no!", he said sadly, "What will I do now? I can't fly with a broken wing".

"Don't worry", said the Unicorn, "I can fix your wing".

And then the unicorn touched the tip of its golden horn against the wing of the Pegasus and the horn started to glow all kinds of bright colours as a magical healing power poured out of it, healing the bones within the wing until all the pain was gone and the pegasus could use it to fly again.

"Oh Unicorn!", said the Pegasus smiling, "I don't know why you want to fly so badly because your horn is much more special than my wings".

That made the unicorn feel so proud of her horn and after that she wasn't jealous of the Pegasus anymore.

The Flying Unicorn

Mario was a unicorn. He was a very special unicorn, and his tribe considered him one of the greatest creatures in the world, for Mario had wings, and he could fly.

Great big gossamer wings the color of moonlight, could take him soaring into the air above, his white body gleaming in the sun at day, and sparkling in the moon-and star-light at night.

he was a happy and good-natured animal and made friends with everyone, even humans. he liked little children, who always stared at her in wonder and delight. One little boy was his special friend. he lived just outside of the forest that

Mario lived in. His name was Louis and he loved Mario with all his heart.

One day when they were walking in the forest, Louis asked Mario, "Dear Mario, would you please, please, take me up with you into the great big sky? I want to see the world from up there. Please, Mario?"

"Of course, I will, my little friend. Would you like to go now?" Mario asked, looking down at Louis.

"Yes please," Hassan shouted, jumping up and down in excitement.

And so, with Louis on her back, Mario flew off into the air, climbing higher and higher, with the little boy screaming in delight. he held on tightly to and looked down at the ground that seemed so very far away. The houses and trees looked like toys. The river looked like a blue line drawn on one of his drawing pages. Birds flew past his chirping a friendly greeting and he waved at them in return.

Soon it was time to return to the ground, and when she landed and she hugged Mario tightly and said, "Thank you so much, dear friend. That was lovely."

The Flying Unicorn And The Boy

Once upon a time, there lived a unicorn named Mia. She always flew up high because she loved going up so she could see the things down below. One day she saw something that interested her, so she flew down.

She landed on the grass. Then she saw a little boy. His name was Max. He was looking at a tree. There was a bird on the tree. "Hi, I am Mia. What are you doing?". The unicorn said. "Hi, I am Max. I am trying to get the magic apple for my mother. She is really sick". Max said. "So it can cure her".

But the bird was guarding the tree so Max could not get the apple. After a while, Max turned to the unicorn. "Do you have magic?" Max asked. "Yes, I do." Mia said. "Can you chase the bird away please?". Max said "Yes, I can". The unicorn replied. Then the Mia pointed her horn at the bird and said "Chase bird! Go bird! Fly away!" and then the bird was gone. "Thank you very much!" Max said, and picked an apple and off he went.

Max was planning a surprise for Mia for helping him. Three days later, the unicorn saw Max and his little brother near a new, lovely and colorful stable. "Hi, Max!". "Hi, Mia!".

Max said. "I have something to give you". Then Max led Mia to the beautiful stable. "My mother is getting better. We thank you for helping us. This is a present for you". Max said. "Wow, it is a beautiful stable. I love it. Thank you!". Mia said and smiled cheerfully. "I have been always wanted a stable". "You're very welcome!". Max said.

The following day, Max saw Mia again. "Hello, Mia!". "Hello, Max!". They both said. "Are you hungry, Mia?" "Yes, I am." Mia said. "Well, there is an apple tree near my house even though you can't see it. Do you want to pick some apples to eat?". Max asked. "Of course, I do. Let's go there". Mia said. Then they walked while talking until they came to the apple tree. Max grabbed two apples and they ate. When they were done with eating, they said goodbye to each other and went home. From then on, they will be best friends.

A Beautiful Waterfall

A beautiful waterfall of white light is flowing downon you. It flows down on your head, helping yourhead to relax. You feel your head relaxing. Itmoves down over your neck and shoulders. Yourneck and shoulders are relaxing. Now it flowsdown over your arms. You feel your arms relaxing.It flows down your back. Your back is letting goand relaxing. It flows over your chest and stom-ach, helping your chest and stomach relax. Youfeel your chest and stomach relax. It moves downover your legs and feetletting go and relaxing. The beautiful waterfall ofwhite light is flowing over your whole body. Youare very peaceful and relaxed. and feet. You feel your legs and feetletting go and relaxing. The beautiful waterfall ofwhite light is flowing over your whole body. Youare very peaceful and relaxed.

Lotus Seed

Imagine that you are a lotus seed buried beneath amuddy lotus pond. There is mud all around you,and you can feel them clearly. Above you, abovethis muddy pool of dirt, mud and filth, are sun-shine and air. You are not disheartened as youbegin your journey towards the surface.With a determined heart, you begin to wiggle inthe earth. You grow roots deep, deep into the mud.Your little stem grows up slowly. Suddenly, "pop"you are out of the mud! Your stem grows higherand higher, taller and taller. You rise up slowly, fighting against the muddy water. All of a sudden, you are out of the muddy pond! You reach up towards the warm sun, shining down on you. Your lotus bud begins to grow on top of your stem. It expands and grows larger and larger, finally bursting into full bloom. A white lotus flower. You stand beautifully above the muddy water, not dirt-ied by the mud from which you grow. You are white, fragrant and beautiful. Everyone who saw you marvelled at your beauty! Your determination to grow out of the muddy pond reminds them of the Buddha and his journey towards Enlightenment. The Buddha, like a lotus, is determined to grow out of the muddy surround-ings, that is the defilements and sufferings of life. He has done all that is to be done and he is show-ing us that we can all do it too. We may have defilements but we all have the potential of grow-ing out of our defilements and achieving wisdom, like the Buddha. You are a beautiful white lotus flower, and your role is to remind people to rise above their defile-ments and sufferings, just as you are arising above the muddy water and not dirtied by the mud from which you grow.

Stick Of Incense

Imagine that you are a stick of incense. Someonecomes along and lights up a matchstick. The per-son puts the little flame to the tip of the incense.Immediately, you are burning away. As you are burning, your body gives off a lovelyfragrant smell. This fragrance spreads through theair and brings joy and happiness to people's heart. The person then offers you to the Buddha. You arebeing put into an incense pot. You stand happilyin the incense pot because you know that youhave an important role to play. Your fragrancesymbolises the fragrance of pure moral conduct.And this reminds people to cultivate good conduct.This fragrance spreads in all directions through-out the world.As you are burning away, you also remind peopleto try and burn away their bad, unkind or selfish thoughts. They should try to be like you, burningaway their selfish acts and bringing fragrance andhappiness to the world. Let every breath, thateveryone breathes out into the world be full ofsweetness and love. Continue to spread your fra-grance in all directions.

Color Of Rainbow

Feel your body becoming lighter and lighter. Seeall the colours of the rainbow. Feel your bodybecoming all of the colours of the rainbow. Slowly, you are now giving out red colour. Yourwhole body becomes red colour. Feel yourself giv-ing out energy and strength. You are now full ofenergy and strength. Slowly, you are now giving out orange colour. Yourwhole body becomes orange colour. Feel yourselfgiving out happiness and joy. You are now full ofhappiness and joy. Slowly, you are now giving out yellow colour. Yourwhole body becomes yellow colour. Feel yourselfgiving out intelligence. You are now full of intelli-gence.

Slowly, you are now giving out green colour. Yourwhole body becomes green colour. Feel yourselfgiving out harmony and friendship. You are nowfull of harmony and friendship. Slowly, you are now giving out blue colour. Yourwhole body becomes blue colour. Feel yourself giv-ing out peace. You are now full of peace. Slowly, you are now giving out indigo colour. Yourwhole body becomes indigo colour. Feel yourselfgiving out gentleness. You are now full of gentle-ness. Slowly, you are now giving out violet colour. Yourwhole body becomes violet colour.

Feel yourselfgiving out beauty and self-respect. You are nowfull of beauty and self-respect.You are the rainbow, your colours are going outeverywhere. Feel yourself getting bigger and big-ger, your colours going out further and further,until they cover up this whole room, then furtheruntil they cover the whole country, and still fur-ther until they cover the whole world. As youspread out all the colours, you are also spreading out energy, happiness, intelligence, friendship,peace, gentleness and beauty. You spread outeven farther and become even bigger. Now yourcolours of light are spreading throughout thewhole universe. You are as big as the whole uni-verse, your colours of light shining out in everdirection in space and touching all of space.Slowly, all the colours changed into a stream ofwhite light. This white light is now flowing downthe top of your head down to your heart. Feel allthe white light going into your heart.

Lotus Candle

Imagine that you are a lotus candle. Someonewalks toward you and lightsyour wick. You arenow giving out a small glow of orange light.Slowly, your whole body becomes an orange colour.Feel yourself giving out warm orange light. Some-one lifts you up and places you on the shrine table. Your warm orange light is like the brightness ofwisdom. You are now shining brightly, as bright asyou can be, to drive away the darkness of igno-rance. Your light symbolizes the Buddha's teach-ing. His teachings help and guide us when we arein darkness. When we behave badly and get angry,it is as if we are in darkness. We need the light ofthe Buddha's teaching to help us. Your light helps to remind people not to remain indarkness but to brighten themselves with theBuddha's teaching.

You are the bright orange light. Feel yourselfexpanding, your light going out further and fur-ther, until it shines through the whole temple,then further until it shines through the wholecountry, and still further until it covers thewhole world. You are as big as the whole worldand your light breaks through all the darknessand your light shines out in every direction. Yourlight of wisdom is touching all of space. Continuegiving out orange light in every direction.

Feeling Of Joy

Imagine a feeling of joy. You feel an opening in thetop of your head. You feel joy floating in throughthe opening in the top of your head. It fills up your head and neck. It fills your shoul-ders and arms. The joy floats down into your chestand your heart. Your heart is so full of joy. The joygently floats on into your stomach and on intoyour back. It floats into your legs and feet. Everypart of your body is full of joy. You are so full of joy, it begins to spread outbeyond your body. It spreads out to everyone inour classroom. It reaches beyond the classroomfarther and farther until it spreads over the wholeof Singapore. It spreads out to the whole earth,and continues to spread out even further into theuniverse — beyond the planets, beyond the stars,farther and farther. The whole universe is filledwith your joy.

A Beautiful Flower

Imagine that you are a beautiful flower. What kind of flower are you? See the colour of your petals. Appreciate that you are now a beautiful flower.Someone comes along and buys you from theflower shop. She puts you into a vase filled withwater. You are gently sucking up the water andblooming more beautifully than before. You arefresh and sending off a sweet fragrance. The ladyputs you on the table and offers you to theBuddha. You stand beautifully in the vase, bring-ing joy and happiness to people's hearts whenthey see you. One day has passed. Slowly, the colour of yourpetals becomes dull. You are no longer sending offa sweet fragrance. Your petals become witheredand discoloured. You are ugly and faded.

Although you are a withered flower, you are stillhappy in your heart. You know that you have animportant role to play. Your role is to remindpeople of the Buddha's teaching that all things areimpermanent. All things are constantly goingthrough change. Everyone's body too, like yourpetals, will wither and pass away. Everyoneshould keep impermanence in mind and live in the present.

Clean Water

Imagine that you are now pure clean water. Some-one comes along and gently put you into a smallbowl. The person then offers you to the Buddha. You rest happily in the bowl knowing that youhave an important role to play. You symbolisepurity, clarity and calmness. You remind people topractise the Buddha's teachings, which is con-stantly cleansing their minds. Water is used to clean away dirt. When everyonesees you, they are happy and joyful. This isbecause they are reminded that they can washaway the filth of their minds. They should washaway selfish and unkind thoughts and be cleanand pure like you. The Buddha is someone free from dirty defilementslike desire, ill-will and ignorance. We should all be like the Buddha, who does not have any dirt ofdefilements but only purity in his mind.

A Dream Come True

Once upon a time, there lived a girl named Sara, who wished to see a unicorn. One day, she dreamt that she was riding a unicorn. When she woke up, she said, "It was just a dream."

The next day, she was sad because she wanted to see a real unicorn. When she was playing outside, her mother said, "Come children. It's lunch time," and Sara said, "ok." But just then a unicorn appeared and said, "You want to ride with me?" and Sara said, "sure." When she ride on it, she said, "You are my pet," and then she lived happily ever after.

Save The Unicorn

"Unicorn! Unicorn!" shouted Kia. "I've just seen a unicorn!"

Everyone in the marketplace turned to stare at her. Her father, Jed the blacksmith, dropped his hammer in amazement.

"A unicorn? Impossible! No-one's seen a unicorn round here in twenty years."

"Well, I did!" insisted Kia. "It was down in the forest, by the pool."

"Are you sure?"

"Of course I'm sure! It had a horn as long as my arm. It was so beautiful!" sighed Kia. The unicorn had been standing quite still, gazing down into the water. It had looked like a statue carved from moonlight.

"What's that? You found a unicorn?"

At the booming voice behind her, Kia spun round. Sir Crabcut was striding across the market square.

Sir Crabcut lived in the castle. He was as broad and impatient as a bull - a bull with ginger whiskers. They bristled fiercely when he spoke; or rather, when he bellowed. He only had one tone of voice, which was loud.

Right now, his eyes were bulging with disbelief.

"You?" he thundered. "You found a unicorn? A scruffy brat like you?"

Kia dropped a curtsey. "Yes, indeed, sir," she said proudly.

"Hmph! What did you do with it?"

"I didn't do anything," said Kia. "I just crept away, so as not to frighten it."

"What?" he roared. "You silly girl, why didn't you catch it? I could have added it to my collection!"

"Collection?" Kia was bemused.

Then, with a gasp of horror, she realised what he meant. Once, peeping through the castle window, she'd seen a host of glass eyes staring back. Animals' heads were ranged around the wall. There were stags, wild-eyed wolves, surly bears, and even a small, sad dragon.

"Come to think of it," snorted Sir Crabcut, "a grubby little peasant-girl like you could never catch a unicorn. But it's just what I need for my collection! It'll look perfect over the fireplace."

He turned and bellowed at the crowd. "Well, what are you waiting for, men? Fetch the horses! Get your weapons and saddle up! We're going hunting!"

"What?" cried Kia. "You can't!"

"I most certainly can. Jump to it!" snapped Sir Crabcut, and the crowd jumped to it and began to run for their horses.

Kia caught at her father's arm. "You mustn't let him catch the unicorn!" she begged.

The blacksmith scratched his head. "I don't like it, but how can we stop him? Sir Crabcut's our master. If we disobey him he'll clap us in chains."

"Well, he's not my master," declared Kia. "If you can't save the unicorn, I will. I'll drive it away before he gets there. Can I borrow a horse?"

"Sir Crabcut will take all the fast horses. But you can have old Molly, if you like. Be careful!"

Kia hurried to the field where Molly the old grey mare was grazing, and scrambled up onto her back.

"Run like the wind!" she urged.

Molly could not run like the wind. She could trot like a gentle breeze. She was balding and scarred, and wheezy from many years of pulling carts, but she was always happy to carry Kia.

Down to the woods she ambled, with Kia anxiously glancing over her shoulder. There was no sign of Sir Crabcut... yet.

Inside the forest, all was still and silent. A carpet of leaves swallowed the sound of Molly's hooves.

The trees reached out with long grasping fingers to pull Kia's hair and tug at her clothes: but she urged Molly on, until at last she saw a glimmer like a star caught in the black net of trees.

She dismounted from Molly to creep closer. She hadn't been mistaken. There stood the unicorn, poised and graceful, by the pool.

Kia caught her breath. She couldn't help murmuring, "Oh, it's lovely!"

The unicorn looked up at her, then back at its reflection in the water. It tilted its head elegantly.

"Yes, I am rather magnificent, aren't I?" it said.

"You can talk!"

"Well, of course. All unicorns can talk. We're very clever beasts."

"I've come to warn you!" said Kia.

"Oh?"

"You've got to leave!" she urged. "Leave now! Run away before Sir Crabcut comes to catch you."

"Catch me? Really? I don't think so."

"He wants to cut your head off and stick it on his wall!"

The unicorn sniffed and tossed its silky mane. "Hah! No-one can catch me. We unicorns are far too clever to get caught."

"Why, I could have caught you just now!" cried Kia. "You let me walk right up to you. I could catch you easily!"

The unicorn looked down its sleek white nose at her. "No, you couldn't."

"Could!"

"Couldn't," said the unicorn, glancing down again at its reflection with a complacent smile.

Kia whipped off her cloak and threw it over the unicorn's head. As the unicorn wheeled and stamped, she held on tight. "See? I've caught you."

"No, you haven't," said the cloak in a muffled voice. "I wasn't trying. You couldn't catch me if I was trying."

Kia unwrapped her cloak. "All right," she said, with gritted teeth. "Start trying!"

The unicorn galloped off around the pool. "Hah! You can't catch me now!" it whinnied.

But Kia marched away in the other direction, under the trees.

Taking an apple from her pocket, she laid it on the ground. She climbed the tree above it and draped herself along a low branch. Then she called out,

"Hey, unicorn! Here's a lovely fresh apple!"

"Where?"

"Just here. Mmm, looks delicious!"

Eagerly the unicorn trotted over.

As it nosed at the apple, Kia dropped from her branch onto its back. Although it bucked and snorted, it couldn't throw her off.

"See?" she panted. "I caught you again."

"I let you catch me," retorted the unicorn sulkily. "I knew it was a trick. And don't hang on my horn like that: you might break it."

"That's not a bad idea," she said, sliding off its back. "Without your horn, Sir Crabcut would think you were an ordinary horse. Then he'd leave you alone."

But the unicorn squealed indignantly. "An ordinary horse? Moi? And how can you talk about breaking my beautiful horn? They never grow back, you know!"

"Then there's nothing else for it. You've got to run away," said Kia firmly. "Sir Crabcut will be here soon with his men."

The unicorn snorted. "I'm not scared. I can outwit anybody."

"You can't even outwit me!"

"Oh, you don't count. You're just a scruffy little girl," declared the unicorn. It munched up the apple and strolled away.

Kia clenched her fists. She wanted to scream. None the less, she had vowed to save this unicorn, and that was what she would do - whether the unicorn liked it or not.

But time was running out.

Dusk was thickening beneath the trees. The moon was rising, so that a second, fragile moon shimmered in the pool.

Kia was thinking hard. If she could only lure the unicorn over to her again, and somehow harness it, then she could lead it away.

She began to pull long strands of ivy from the trees, and knotted them together to make a rope.

Next, picking up an ash branch, she peeled away the bark until the wood was as smooth and pale as the unicorn's horn.

Then she went to find Molly.

"Molly! Here, girl!" she called softly. The old mare was grazing under the trees. When she trudged over, Kia held the branch against her scarred grey head and tied it carefully into position with some ivy. "There! How do you like being a unicorn?"

Molly shook her head experimentally. The branch stayed in place.

"Hmm. It isn't very realistic," decided Kia, "but then the unicorn isn't very bright. Now stand there, Molly, and don't move!"

She arranged an ivy noose on the ground nearby, and ran off to find the unicorn.

"Oh, do come and look," she called. "I've found another one!"

"Another what?"

"Another unicorn! It's over here. Just follow me!"

The unicorn cantered after her. On seeing Molly, it threw back its head and whinnied joyfully.

"Unicorn! Unicorn!"

As it trotted forward, it placed a foot inside the ivy noose. At once Kia pulled it tight.

"Caught you!"

"No, you didn't," said the unicorn, trying unsuccessfully to free its leg.

"Did!"

"Didn't. I'm just about to get free. Any second now."

"But -"

Kia stopped. There was a crashing of branches, a clashing of swords, and a neighing of horses.

"Any second now, you'll be dead!" she cried. "Quick! There's no time to run. Lie down!"

"How dare you order me about?" huffed the unicorn.

Kia tugged at the noose, and its legs shot up in the air. It landed on its side in the dead leaves, snorting indignantly.

"I have never been so -" it began, before Kia threw her cloak over it.

"Quiet!" she hissed. Swiftly she heaped armfuls of brown leaves over the cloak.

By the time Sir Crabcut and his men rode into the clearing, she was standing innocently in front of a large pile of dead leaves.

"Well?" roared Sir Crabcut. "Where's this unicorn, wretched child?"

"I think it must have gone away," said Kia, hoping the unicorn would not try to stand up. She heard a faint shuffle from the heap of leaves.

Sir Crabcut frowned. Dismounting from his horse, he strode forward, whiskers quivering.

"What's that?" He drew his sword.

"Look!" cried Jed the blacksmith. "Look! A unicorn!" And he pointed - not at the pile of rustling leaves, but in the other direction, towards the pool.

There stood Molly, gazing down into the water. The moonlight painted her grey coat silver. From this distance, the ash stick strapped to her forehead shone as white and sharp as a horn.

Then Molly raised her head, and slipped away into the trees.

"After it! Catch it!" yelled Sir Crabcut. Leaping back on his horse, he set off in pursuit.

The blacksmith and the other riders galloped after him. They hurtled around the pool and into the depths of the forest. Kia was alone.

The unicorn rolled over and sat up, blowing at the leaves. "Hoo! Told you they wouldn't catch me!" it panted.

"No," said Kia miserably. "They'll catch Molly instead. It won't take them long. She can't run very fast or very far. And then Sir Crabcut will be furious. He might kill her! And it's all your fault."

She sat down in the dead leaves and burst into tears.

After a few moments she felt something nudge against her legs.

The unicorn had lain down beside her. It rested its head on her lap and looked up at her with glistening eyes. One huge silver tear rolled down its face.

"Oh, my," said Kia, and she used her cloak to wipe first the unicorn's face and then her own.

"It's not really your fault," she whispered, sniffing. "It's my fault, for telling Sir Crabcut about you in the first place. I wish I'd never said a word."

"I don't want Molly to get killed," wailed the unicorn. "I'll go and give myself up right now." It began to lurch to its feet.

"No, you mustn't. Stop!" For Kia could hear the rumble of returning hooves. She pushed the protesting unicorn back down into the leaves and covered it up again.

Then she hurried forward to meet the horsemen cantering back through the twilight.

Sir Crabcut held Molly's reins in his hairy fist. Furiously he dragged the horse into the moonlit clearing. She was wheezing dreadfully and limping. The ash stick dangled from her shoulders in a tangle of ivy.

Sir Crabcut seized the stick and waved it at Kia.

"What do you know about this, then, eh?" he bellowed.

Kia gazed up at him, biting her lip. She did not know what to say.

"Well?"

It was her father Jed who answered. "It's nothing to do with her! You can see she's as surprised as the rest of us. It's just somebody's idea of a joke. It fooled us all."

"Hmph!" growled Sir Crabcut. "Silly little girl, who can't tell the difference between a unicorn and a carthorse!"

"I - I'm very sorry, sir," said Kia.

"I might have known it was a waste of time," he grunted. "There are no unicorns round here any more. It's twenty years since I last saw a unicorn in this forest - and I would have caught it, too, if its horn hadn't broken off in my trap and let it get away."

"Well, I expect it must have told the other unicorns," suggested Kia, "and they were all too scared of you to ever come back."

"Hmph! Scared of me? Yes, that's very likely." Sir Crabcut twirled his ginger moustache.

Kia put her hand on Molly's back. She could feel the old mare's flanks heaving breathlessly. "Are you going to chop off Molly's head?"

"What would I want with an old horse's head on my wall? It would look very vulgar. I only collect rare and special animals."

"I hear somebody spotted a griffin the other week," said Jed the blacksmith casually.

Sir Crabcut's eyes brightened. "A griffin? Where?"

"Oh, miles away. Too far for you to go."

"It's never too far for a griffin! Now that would look good on my wall! I'll have to set up an expedition." Sir Crabcut let go of Molly at last. "Well, come on, men! Enough dawdling. I want my dinner."

He set off at a canter towards the castle. His tired men trooped after him. Only the blacksmith stayed behind.

"A griffin should keep him busy for a while," he chuckled.

"I hope so. I was so worried about Molly!" Kia threw her arms around the old mare's neck and hugged her. "Brave girl, leading them away like that! It's just as well Sir Crabcut's even more stupid than the unicorn."

"Who are you calling stupid?"

The unicorn rose up haughtily. A rustling drift of leaves fell from its back.

"Well, fancy thinking Molly's horn was real!" said Kia.

"Do you think I don't know another unicorn when I see one?" It walked gracefully over to Molly and nuzzled against her shoulder.

"Oh, honestly! Couldn't you see it was only..."

Kia paused. Slowly she reached up and stroked Molly's grey head. It was growing too dark to see clearly, but her fingers felt a hard, round scar right in the middle of Molly's forehead.

"Dad?" she whispered. "Where did we get Molly?"

Jed shrugged. "I don't know where she came from. She just wandered into our field one day, when I was a boy, twenty years ago. Now, what are we going to do with this unicorn?"

"You're not doing anything with me." The unicorn stamped impatiently. "I'm taking Molly home."

"Molly?" asked Jed, bewildered.

The old horse sighed. Then, in a cracked, husky voice that had not been used for years, Molly wheezed, "I tried to go home... but I forgot the way."

"Oh, poor Molly!" Really, Kia thought, stroking her ragged mane, unicorns weren't very bright at all.

"Then it's lucky that I know the right path," said the unicorn. "I'll show you now. Come on!"

Kia stood back with her father and watched the pair of them prance around the pool. Molly followed the younger unicorn eagerly, tossing her stiff old head in joy. The moonlight bathed them both in liquid silver.

Shining like a pair of stars, they trotted away beneath the trees. Slowly the light faded until it was no more than a glimmer in the dusk.

But just before they disappeared for good, Kia heard a last, faint whinny echo through the woods:

"You can't catch me...!"

The Mystical Unicorn

Once upon a time there was a beautiful princess. While she was out walking in her magical kingdom she met a unicorn. The unicorn was very surprised because they are very shy and timid creatures. "Wow, how beautiful," the princess said. "Oh my goodness," neighed the Unicorn. The princess walked closer to the Unicorn very carefully. "Do not be afraid Mr. Unicorn." The Unicorn said, "My name is Sheldon, what is your name?" "My name is Margaret." "We will be very good friends Margaret." And they were.

Years passed and the two became close friends. Margaret invited the unicorn to her house for dinner one night. The Unicorn decided that it would be alright as long as no one would see him. In order for him to be invisible he had to use magic. The magic from his horn turned rainbow and from that moment the only one who could see him was Margaret. While Margaret and Sheldon were in town they saw the handsome prince. Margaret loved the prince. She asked Sheldon to make him fall in love with her. Sheldon agreed.

The Stinky Unicorn

Once there was a stinky unicorn named Princess. who walked by a house? it looked like a pink castle and she went in. She looked through every room to find the bedroom. because she was so sleepy. The walls were all pink, with a big fluffy bed with lots of pillows. It was perfect for a queen. Princess the Stinky Unicorn got into that big comfy bed and took a nap.

Princess woke up to a grumbly stomach. She headed down to the kitchen to make herself a snack. Suddenly the door opened. the Royal Family was home. They smelt something gross. "Eww. what is that smell? Princess Haley asked. They followed the smell all the way up the stairs to the bedroom.

'Someone was in my bed and now it smells! Princess Haley cried. 'We can clean it up; Queen Mommy said. I'm not helping. Way too smelly. Princess Haley said. pinching her nose. I don't blame you. Let's go to the kitchen and get the cleaning supplies. Queen Nanna said.

The Royal Family made their way to the kitchen. The smell was in the kitchen too! They couldn't believe their eyes. there was a unicorn sitting at their kitchen table. -What are you doing? Get out of our house- King Babba ordered. -Go back to your own home: Princess Paley added.

I don't have a home, - Prince the Stinky Unicorn said sadly. "But everyone has a home. - Princess Haley said. don't. I was so tired and hungry. I'm sorry. - "You can stay here. This could be your home. Please, mommy. Princess Haley said, pleading to her mom.

-Well. no Royal Family is complete without a Royal Pet. It does not get more royal than a unicorn. Queen Mommy said warmly. -No. no way. Not until she is no longer stinky. Queen Nanna ordered. -I can give her a bath: Princess Haley said. -You start on the bath and start on the room: Queen Mommy said. -King Babba will help you: Queen Nanna added.

"I can really Stay? Princess the Stinky Unicorn asked. Only if you get clean. - Queen Hanna said, "Come on, I'll help you: - Princess Haley said. Princess Haley and King Babba took Princess the Stinky Unicorn upstairs to the bath. Princess could not have been any happier. She finally has a home and a new loving family.

After a nice warm bath and lots of bubbles. Princess was no longer the stinky unicorn. Now she was Princess the Royal Unicorn. The End.

Unicorns And Rainbows

What do you think of when you first hear the word unicorns? Rainbows and horses with horns? Well, that's not what they are like. Unicorns aren't just pretty and full of happiness. They can talk and fly and change colors and sizes and are overall amazing. But they hold a secret, a secret that can change our lives forever. We ARE the unicorns. Yes, you heard right, we all are unicorns. And we can fly. And do anything you can imagine. The only catch is, this is in our imagination. We can be anything we want to be. If you wanted, you could be a pixie and a rock star, all in your imagination.

So just remember, the mind is a powerful thing. It can create anything. Take my words into consideration, my friends. Use your imagination, and anything is possible.

Unicorn And Lollipop

Unicorn was extremely bored so she decided to travel to Rainbow Falls. Once she reached her destination, Unicorn heard a screaming noise coming from a little gingerbread house. She ate through the delicious chocolate door and saw some idiot sucking on a lollipop. Unicorn rescued the lollipop "moooo moo mooo" she asked "My name is Empedestrious, but you can call me Lollipop" the lollipop replied. "Mooo!" Unicorn exclaimed. They both danced over to Sprinkles, The Queen of Unicorns which is the most powerful unicorn ever. "I've been stalking you Unicorn and I see my stupid good for nothing unicorn-in-training finally saved a victim of citizenship. It's hard to say this Unicorn, but Good job!" Then the Unicorn of Unicorns (Blu) trotted over and gave Unicorn a new sparkly horn as a reward. The President of Unicorns (Bubbles) then flew over and said in a harsh tone "Congrats, you unworthy little donkey". After that, not so proud yet proud moment, Unicorn and Lollipop ventured off to Bubblelandia, where they ran into the Giant Cookie who feeds on Unicorn bacon flesh. "Mo mooo oh crap" Unicorn muttered.

What do we do" Lollipop asked "moo mo eat it" Unicorn replied hungrily. "Meh hungry" Lollipop agreed. They chomped down on the Cookie, it tasted a lot like pizza... weird. After that Unicorns stomach was extended so it dragged when she walked "It looks like your preggo" Lollipop laughed. Unicorn stuck her tongue out at him then little rabid fruit snacks waddled up to them. "Awe I'll call u peachy, u dandy, and u vicious" Lollipop announced. Peachy had sharp fangs hanging from his little gummy mouth. Dandy had red evil looking eyes and Vicious had a sweet smile and cute dimples. The names matched perfectly! Peachy sprinted at Lollipop and bit his stick which held his rainbow colored head. Unicorn got angry then ate off Peachy and Dandy's head. Vicious waddled up to Unicorn and gave her a hug, that monster! "M'oo mooo moo moooo I'll deal with you later said the unicorn" Unicorn snapped at Vicious, then helped Lollipop. "Hey Unicorn have you lost weight" Lollipop asked loopy. Ah man the poison already got to his head.

Vicious is so nice" Lollipop murmured. That poison is obviously screwing up his little lollipop brain. Unicorn started sucking the poison off of Lollipops head. After a while Lollipop was back to normal "what happen" he asked "moo mooooo moooooo mooo you called Vicious nice" Unicorn explained scoffing at Vicious's name. Lollipop gasped "Mo moo moo moo mo mooooo moo moooo oh and you got bit by Peachy and Dandy" Unicorn added. "Oh well things happen, but I can't believe I said Vicious was nice just look at him" Lollipop said. They both looked at Vicious who was currently chewing on his own arm, how disgusting. When Vicious realized they were staring at him, he waddled over to them and said "hold meh, hold meh". He reached his arms up to Unicorn "Kill it, kill it" Lollipop screeched. Unicorn did as he said and repeatedly jabbed her horn into Vicious, then the sun beat down on him and he melted. Praise the Queen of Unicorns! "Finally that disgusting thing is gone" Lollipop cheered. Oh happy times, oh happy times!

Moo mooo mooo mooooooooo moooo mo mooo, mooo mo mo moooo mooo Now that that disgusting thing is gone, lets go to Candy Lane" Unicorn exclaimed. They walked stupidly over to Candy Lane when a Skittle cop stopped them. "You do know your stupidity has affected the whole neighborhood" she said. Both Unicorn and Lollipop looked around and saw everyone in the little town sticking their tongue out like Unicorn always does and hopping on one foot cuz Lollipop does. "You made the whole town dumb" Skittle cop explained angrily. Lollipop looked at Unicorn and said "there's only one way to get out of this" Unicorn nodded...

Unicorn and Lollipop started eating the almighty delicious Skittle cop. Afterwards they stumbled into the most epic fish ever..... NEMO! "Whoa what are you doing here" Lollipop asked "ca nt br e ath" Nemo gasped out "sorry, we don't speak arthritis" Lollipop replied then walked away as Nemo called "Don't touch the butt" then died. "Moooo mooooooo m mooo mo mo mo mo moooooo mooo sorry lollipop I have to go to my rainbow home" " It's fine, see ya tomorrow" Lollipop said then hopped away. As Unicorn made her way through a dark cave she saw an awesome ninja dude "sup" he asked "moooooo mooo, mooo moooooo moo mooo moooooooo moooooo nothing much, just watching you kill innocent civilians" Unicorn replied simply "haha you talk funny" the ninja guy said "mooo moooo mooo m moo moo moooooo moooooo what's your name I bet its something awesome like killer" Unicorn asked curiously.........

My name is Mr. Ninja Dude Awesomeness" Ninja guy replied "Mooo mooo mooo best name ever" Unicorn said in awe. They walked towards Unicorns home together when all of a sudden a hole in the ground swallows them up.

Unicorn looked around and noticed they were in water. "Look over there a pineapple" Mr. Ninja Dude Awesomeness exclaimed. They swam over to where the pineapple was and knocked on the door that was attached. A sponge with squared pants answered it "Hello" he said. Unicorn realized it was Spongebob Squarepants from her most favorite show ever. He invited them in and as soon as she entered a bunch of things yelled "suprise". Unicorn looked around and saw Lollipop, Sprinkles, Blu, Bubbles, Peachy, Dandy, Nemo, Patrick Star and dun,dun,dun..... Vicious. "Should we kill them" Mr. Ninja Dude Awesomeness asked "moo moo mooo moooo mooo mooo moooooo mooooooo mooo not all of them just that freaky looking one" Unicorn explained pointing towards Vicious. After Mr. Ninja Dude Awesomeness returned he said "Oh by the way my real name is just Mr". That killed the mood! Then Lollipop hopped over and asked "So how do you like the party" "moo mooo moo moooo mooo moo mooo its cool but what is it for" Unicorn asked. " It's to celebrate Leapfaresen Day, oh and it's for our celebration of Broski and Broseph Day!" Lollipop explained.

In the end Lollipop and Unicorn got married moved to Bikini Bottom and had 200 kids!

Shine Your Light

Gently close your eyes and softly repeat, "I am still."

Notice your body relax instantly and easily. Allow your body to sink down in your bed further and further, as your muscles become soft and limp. It feels so comfortable.

Your body just seems to relax more and more with each and every word you hear.

Imagine now a small sparkle somewhere deep inside your heart. This small sparkle begins to glow brighter now, and you feel it reaching up and expanding out.

The glow becomes brighter and brighter filling up your chest. You feel the warmth spreading out touching your tummy, your shoulders.... getting bigger and bigger.... getting brighter and brighter, glowing all the way down to your toes.

Now feel your whole body glowing like a radiant star shining out. This wonderful light is your light – your shining light – your personal brilliance. It is all the love in your heart. It is the sum of your possibilities – and your possibilities are endless.

Shine your light wherever you go. Sharing your light makes others happy, and it makes you happy as well. It's a wonderful feeling to share your light, and by doing so, you become a good example to them.

When you shine your light brightly, it lets others know that it is okay for them to shine their light brightly too. When we all do this, it makes the world a more beautiful, peaceful place.

Sharing your light can be as simple as sharing your smile, or doing a kind deed. Hold a happy thought about someone, or send a happy wish to someone who is feeling sad. It can mean helping someone who is younger than you, or not as strong as you.

All of this is shining your light, and you will discover a wonderful warm, fuzzy feeling inside your heart when you do this.

This wonderful feeling comes from doing what you were created to do – feeling and spreading love and joy. Sharing your light means sharing the real you and being who you truly are. It means standing up for what is right and making the choices that feel right in your heart.

Now, allow that bright light inside to become like a gentle shower of fireworks.

See how beautiful and amazing you are?

You light up the sky!

As the fireworks sizzle and flare down, imagine your brilliant light touching the heart of every person you know and will meet. They feel happier just because they know you. How wonderful and blessed life is!

Now take in a deep breath and bring back all the good feelings you have right now with you as you slowly stretch your body. Open your eyes when you're ready. You've done an amazing job!

Unicorn Village

Once Upon a Time... In the really big city, there is a Girl named Teressa or you can call her Ressa. She is playing with her friends Krystal, Kailey, and Chloe. They called RKKC at School like a Squad. When its Saturday RKKC play in Chloe's House. Ressa see a weird place and Ressa Said "guys what is that place?". Chloe said "where?". Ressa said "over there!". Krystal Said "let's go there!". Kailey said "i don't think that is a great idea". Chloe, Ressa, and Krystal Shout "Come on Kailey!". Kailey said "okay". Let's Go! And They are going to the weird place and they see weird bottle say "drink me" and They drink the Liquid from the bottle and..... they feel weird.

They meet Unicorn name "Magicorn". Magicorn said "hi guys welcome To Unicorn Village!" And RKKC Shout

"Ahhhhhhhhh!" Magicorn said "Don't be afraid, By the Way Who are you guys?" Ressa said " We are from Chloe's House and we see a big purple hole and we here." Magicorn said "Can you introduce your friend?" Ressa said "Sure! This Krystal that has a blonde hair. This Kailey you can call her Kay by The Way, Krystal and Kailey are siblings. This is Chloe that has a brown hair. Phew that was a lot." Magicorn Said "You all call me Magic okay?" RKKC said "okay!" Magic show all the Unicorn Village.

Krystal said "I'm so hungry" Magic Said "Uhh, I have a milk only" Krystal said "What! How about the food?!" Magic said "Unicorn only drink milk" Krystal said "Magic, can you stay here for a while, we want to talk for a while?" Magic said "Okay I'll wait" Krystal said " What we gonna do, there is no way to get back in our real life!" Chloe said " I know right!" Kailey said " Aha! How about i will talk to Magic and I want to see a Unicorn Secret Room!" Krystal, Chloe, and Ressa said "No, Magic gonna be so suspicious about us!" Kailey said "okay, let's sneak to the Unicorn's Secret Room" Everyone said "Let's Go!"

And They see the green bottle liquid and they see in Magic liquid Menu and the green is for get back to real life! They drink it and they get back at the house right away"

Krystal was really bored and Kailey also bored. They Call their friends Chloe and Ressa. Chloe came to Krystal's house. Ressa can't come because she is busy. Krystal,Kay, and Chloe went swim,eat,and play. Chloe said "I really want to go the Unicorn Village." Kay said "uhh! I don't want to, Unicorns are weird and I don't like unicorns at all!" Krystal and Chloe shout "WHAT?!" Krystal said "hey you lil sis! Unicorns are amazing. You're just jealous because unicorns are colorful!" Kay shout "No, I'm not! Why are so mean to be it's my opinion!" Chloe said "Ulala, here's come the Sisters Wars." Kay and Krys don't like each other.

The next Morning, Kay came to Krystal's room to say sorry. Krys and Kay now are good sisters. Kay said " I'm sorry because Unicorns are amazing now for me." Krystal said "yeah that's okay, i guess you are the Unicorn Lover!" Krym said "yup!" Kay and Krystal were ate breakfast. They ate Egg and Fish. They play together and Ressa call Krystal. Ressa Said in the phone "Hi guys, Im so sorry, because today is my birthday and i forgot to give invatation to you. Can you come quick?" Krystal shout "Ha! Well, that's okay Ressa." Ressa said "Chloe come too!" Kay said "Okay We will be there. They ride a car and they arrived.

Chloe said "Hi!" Kay and Krys said "Hi!"

Ressa said "Hi Krys and Kay! I thought you guys didn't come! Im glad you guys come to my birthday party!" Krys said "Yeah!" Roxy is a mean girl. Roxy said "Hello RKKC aka Worm Squad!" Everybody laughed. Chloe said "Hello!

I like worm you little kiddo!" Kay,Krys, and Ressa Reply "Yeah! We are." Roxy said "Whatever you Lame Trash." Reddy is a mean boy. Reddy said "Roxy, let's go!" Roxy dumped birthday muffin to Chloe's head. Chloe mad and she need to do Revenge on Roxy. Chloe said "That's too easy how about i put four muffins in row!" Chloe dumped muffin to Roxy's head. Reddy said "Well, RKKC VS COOL QUADS!" Krystal and Kay Shout "We are not scare!" The Muffin Wars started. Chloe ask to Ressa "That's okay right?" Ressa said to Chloe "Of course!" Reddy said to Chloe "Stop you Chloe! Roxy is way more better than you, Roxy is more stylish and Pretty, You look like a pig!" Chloe said to Ressa "Ressa! Did you invited them?!" Ressa said to Chloe "No, I'm not. So Weird." Ressa said "Hey you Roxy and Reddy guess what?! I'm gonna kick you guys from my birthday party. You are ruined my birthday party!" Krys said "You two get out!" Kay said "Or not Ressa's parents gonna kick you out! Reddy said "I'm not scared!" Ressa said "Well, Try this time!" Ressa called Roxy and Reddy's Mom. Roxy said "What?! Ugh! I'm sick of you guys!" Reddy said "You're good!" Roxy and Reddy leave The Party.

Ressa said to Roxy "Can you go to Museum?" Roxy Replied "okay." Ressa called Chloe, Krys, and Kay.

At weekend, they decided to go to Museum. They saw so many wonderful things. Roxy said "Guys, What is this?"

Kay said "I don't know." The Bottle say "Unicorn World." Krys said "Let's drink it!" Everbody said "Totally!" They saw really weird thing and that was a Unicorn!" Roxy said "Hi, Who are you?" The Unicorn name is Magic. Magic was in the Unicorn Village, But Magic moved to the Unicorn's big city called "Pastel-Land." Magic said "My name is Magic." Ressa, Chloe, Kay, and Krys Shouted "MAGIC! DO YOU STILL REMEMBER US?!" Magic said "RKKC right?" Chloe said "Yes." Magic said "Why this girl (Roxy) is over here." Krys said "It's our new friend, Roxy." Magic said "Okay." And they live happily together.

The Magical Adventure Of A Unicorn

There once was a unicorn named Ulanda She was a special rainbow unicorn. She had a magical power of "Wishes" Its a really hard and responsible power to have There was a magical flower That if a human finds a flower he will have 3 wishes becoming true.

There were many other unicorns with powers All the unicorns had owners who were fairies They lived in a galaxy where nobody will find them Ulanda also had an owner her name was Bruno. Ahe was the smallest in the kingdom to have a horse Usually fairies get horses when they are 18 But Bruno was special, she was the daughter Of the The amazing king of fairies the 15" So he allowed her to have a horse at the age of 3 She always wore dresses in colour green and blue Her wings were blue with green dots and lines But the day has came that Ulanda had to go to Earth and make the wishes come true The girl that she came to was a 10 yeard old girl Her name was Amnesia she was a little EMO. She got so pissed that she got a rainbow unicorn It was because she was emo so she made 3 wishes Her first wish was to be rich Her second wish was to be famous like Heyley Williams Her third wish was to be able to fly Ulanda did all the wishes and came back to Justice. It was the first time when Ulanda went to earth So fairy's in Justice made a cake to celebrate it. When Ulanda came back she saw the most amazing cake flying and jumping towards her Like a little kid She was so happy and amazed by how important she was to her friends and family they all had a party all day they ate cakes and danced all night.

But We Can't Do That!

Once, long ago, in a land far, far away, there was a school. But it wasn't just any school. It was a school for dinosaurs and unicorns....

But there was one big problem. The dinosaurs and unicorns didn't talk to each other. They didn't play with each other. They didn't even look at each other.

They didn't get along.

No one knew why. It had been that way for as long as anyone could remember. Diana the dinosaur and Ukey the unicorn were always lonely. They had no other dinosaurs or unicorns to play with.

They sat alone, they ate their lunch alone and they did their school work alone. One day, Diana the dinosaur was sick of having no friends to play with, eat her lunch with or imagine with.

So Diana put on a brave face and made a very risky move. Diana had noticed that Ukey the unicorn was lonely too. So, she took a big breath, walked up to Ukey and softly spoke.

"Hey, I'm Diana the dinosaur and I was wondering if you wanted to play." Ukey replied, "But we can't do that."

"We are both lonely and we could have a lot of fun. We could go on adventures and we could imagine together," Diana said.

"That does sound like a lot of fun," said Ukey.

"Come on!" said Diana, and they ran off hand in hand. "We could go to space," said Diana. "But we can't do that!" replied Ukey. "Come on! Let's go!" said Diana, and they began their journey to space. "3, 2, 1 blast off!" they counted. Before they knew it they were in space. They had so much fun floating, exploring and imagining together.

Suddenly the bell rang.

"See you tomorrow," they said as they ran off home. Once again the two friends met at lunch. "Hey, Ukey," said Diana. "Hi, Diana," replied Ukey. "Do you want to go and play?" said Diana.

"Sure," said Ukey, and the two friends ran off hand in hand. "We could go to Candyland," said Diana. "But we can't do that," replied Ukey. "Come on! Let's go!" said Diana, and they began their journey to Candyland. "Hold on tight!" Diana said.

"3, 2, 1," they counted, and before they knew it they were floating on big pink clouds of candyfloss. The two friends had the best time exploring and eating gummy bears, chocolate and marshmallows until they felt sick!

Suddenly the bell rang.

"See you tomorrow," they said as they ran off home. The next day, the two friends met again at lunch. "Hey, Ukey," said Diana. "Hi, Diana," replied Ukey. "Do you want to go play?" said Diana. "Sure," said Ukey, and the two friends ran off hand in hand. "We could go to Storyland," said Diana. "But we can't do that!" replied Ukey. "Of course we can! Let's go," said Diana, and they began their journey to Storyland. "Hold on tight," Diana said.

"3, 2, 1," they counted, and before they knew it they were surrounded by all their favorite storybook characters. The two friends had the best time meeting Little Red Riding Hood, Humpty Dumpty, Alice in Wonderland, The Three Bears and even Jack came down his beanstalk to say, "Hi!". Once again, the two friends were interrupted by the school bell!

"See you tomorrow," they said as they ran off home. Day after day, their friendship grew stronger as their imaginations let them explore amazing places, where their differences didn't matter.

Day after day, the other dinosaurs and unicorns learned that they could be friends and have more fun together than they ever imagined. Once, long ago, in a land far, far away, there was a school. But it wasn't just any school. It was a school for dinosaurs and unicorns and they got along just fine.

The Horse And The Unicorn

This is Princess Unicorn Cookie. She has white fur and a gold unicorn horn. Princess Unicorn Cookie loves to fly in the sky. Even as animals go, she is quite magical.

When someone needs a bit of magic, her horn turns rainbow. Then, she will sprinkle a dash of magic down below.

Polly the Pony loves to run in green pastures and race her friends, Maria and Beatriz.

Polly has brown fur and is beautiful, but Polly doesn't feel beautiful.

Polly lies under the stars at night.

If only I was a unicorn, I would have white fur and be beautiful, Polly thinks.

High above, Princess Unicorn Cookie knows Polly needs a bit of magic.

I know just the thing, "Polly thinks. She gathers magic from the stars and sprinkles it down below. Polly wakes up in the morning. It begins like any other day until she gets a drink from Lake Sparkle. In the water, Polly sees her reflection. Polly sees that she is no longer a pony, but a unicorn!

Polly spread her wings and flies. Polly sees Princess Unicorn Cookie.

I've got to show Maria and Beatriz my new wings. Polly says.

But Maria and Beatriz are horses, not unicorns! They cannot fly up here, Princess replies. Why can't you make them unicorns, too? Polly asks. I only sprinkle magic dust to these who need it, Princess Unicorn Cookie replies. After Princess Unicorn Cookie says goodbye, Polly has time to think quietly. If I choose to stay a Unicorn, I won't be able to see my friends again, Polly thinks.

She thinks some more.

I won't be able to run wildly in the fields. Even though flying is fun, I love running more!

And so that night, Polly the unicorn makes a magical wish to be a pony once more.

When Polly wakes up, she sees the familiar green fields she loves and knows she is home. I missed you, I missed you too says the two. They play tag in the fields. Polly has a question for her friends.

What makes a pony beautiful?

Polly, some ponies have brown fur. Some ponies have white fur. I have black fur. All furs are beautiful. But there are so many things about you that make you truly beautiful.

Polly, you can run fast. You are a kind friend and tell funny jokes. These are all things that make you truly beautiful.

That night, Polly realize the sprinkle of magic she needed wasn't to become a unicorn. The magic she needed was to know that she is beautiful in a way only Polly the Pony can be.

The Real Unicorn And The Grasshopper In a Jar

There once was a grasshopper, who lived in a jar, He seemed to be stuck, he could not jump very far, Longing to float, flutter, and glide through the grass, It seemed like a long shot, as he stared through the glass, He wished for a miracle, for something to change, He felt like his jar, was more of a cage. Time goes by, and the days get slow, Mr. Grasshopper doesn't have a lot of room to grow, He feels kind of sad, and he's giving up hope, Just then, a great flash, a loud snap, and a glow, Left standing so tall after the bright white light, Is what looks like a horse, with a horn, fit for a knight "Maybe, just maybe, if we try really hard, we could tip it right over, and you'd be freed from the jar, He tilted his head, and bumped into the table, But the jar was too heavy, it just stood there, so stable, "Oh i just think it's too hard, I'll be in here forever, "Don't worry Fred, I'll think of something clever" Charlie thought of ideas, and wondered out loud, "I bet I can break it, with the horn, by my mouth," He aimed for the jar, and picked out a mark, He lowered his horn, and got a head start, He ran into the jar, but it did not break apart, It seems as though Fred, had a broken heart "Never, oh never, will I know what it's like, to climb a great mountain, or see stars at night," "Or dance in the wind, or sink in the snow, or play in the grass, after it has been mowed," "Here's an idea, i will just grab this string, then lower it in, you see what i mean?" He put the string in his mouth, and fished it right in, Fred grabbed onto the string, and he started to grin, But the string was too weak, and it snapped as he climbed, He was back to square one, with sad thoughts in his mind. What would they do, poor Charlie and Fred, They tried all the ideas that they had in their head, Until Fred told Charlie to go on with his life, To go use his magic, and get out of his sight "There it is, that's just it, you've got the ticket, My magic is strong, I can probably just lift it," Fred looked at Charlie, and said "just give up, there's no hope" And right at that moment, the jar began to float It went up really high, and tilted and swaggled, It moved really fast, with bright lights that bedazzled, A boom and a zap, a smack and a crack, From the air to the floor, Fred lands on his back He jumps to his feet, and gives Charlie a high five, The two would be friends, for the rest of their lives!

Dragon and Dinosaurs Stories For Kids

Dragons and Dinosaurs once roamed the Earth millions and millions of years ago. Today, thanks to the efforts of many literatures and arts books, we still get a glimpse of their lives and their looks.

However, how much do we actually know about their personal lives back then? How about a collection of stories from the perspectives of the lives of several of these enticing creatures back then? "Collection of Short Dragons and Dinosaur stories" is written from the perspectives of the different types of dragons and dinosaurs that lived on planet Earth a long time ago. Be prepared to go on a thrilling roller coaster ride of emotions as we travel back in time to get an insight of a possible day in their lives.

Kids are always happy reading about dragons and dinosaurs. Therefore, this collection of their stories will make all the kids more happier reading them.

Start reading this for your kids as you follow the different dragons and dinos on a seemingly normal day of their lives...

The Dragon Bride

"Listen, dragon," began Princess Julia of the Kingdom of Vanarre. Her hands were on her hips, her right toe tapping. "This can't go on."

The Southern Dragon, bigger than a house and with a row of spear point spikes along his spine, looked bemused--as well he might. Julia often had that effect on people. Who else would open parley with a dragon by chiding him like a naughty puppy?

The dragon opened his mouth and sent a stream of flame to incinerate a nearby pine tree which flared like a torch before falling into powdery ash in the intensity of the maintained flame. The dragon blinked in a satisfied manner, then glanced sideways to see how Julia had taken the demonstration of power.

She brushed ash off her wine velvet skirt. "That was very thoughtless. This is a new dress." It laced tightly across her bosom, emphasising her full figure. Julia was a big girl.

An odd rusty sound emerged from the dragon.

Julia tilted her head, listening to the crr-crr-crr, then stared directly into the dragon's sapphire eyes. "You're laughing at me," she accused.

"Yes." The dragon curled its tail comfortably around its body and settled in for the parley. "You have courage, princess, but not a great deal of common sense."

"Rubbish," said Julia robustly. She gave up on her ash ruined velvet skirt and sat down on a chunk of rock. "I'm the practical one of the family."

"Heaven help Vanarre, if that's true." The tip of the dragon's tail twitched like a cat's.

"Humph." Julia snorted, but when she thought of her scatterbrained mum, her romantically minded sisters, her sailing mad and currently lost brother, not to mention her daft but lovable dad...the dragon had a point.

No one had expected her dad to become king. He'd been a younger son and the whole family was content to exist in a crumbling drafty castle, interfering in village affairs and pursuing their odd hobbies. But the unexpected death of both the king and his son--their uncle and cousin--in a coaching accident had propelled the charming but impractical family willy-nilly into court life.

The then royal steward--who had known Julia's dad when he was a boy--had retired on the spot. The remaining members of the royal household went around looking confused, but lately Julia had seen signs that they were being seduced into the madness of her family.

Just the other day she had seen the Sewing Mistress making a vest for her sister Emily's half bald pet parrot. Jake the parrot had been Eric's last gift to the family--and he hadn't considered the language that old bird already knew. If Julia's dad ever wanted to swear at his stuffed shirt royal advisers he just borrowed Jake and let the bird talk. The advisers were soon cussed out of the chamber and Jake rewarded with his favourite treat of sultanas soaked in rum.

"Err-hmm." The Southern Dragon cleared his throat with a rumble like thunder.

"Oh, sorry." Julia often grew distracted when she thought of her family. Really it was Eric's responsibility to parley with the dragon, but Eric was off discovering the Farawy

Islands and currently out of contact somewhere on the uncharted seas.

"You said you had a proposition for me," prompted the dragon.

"I do." Julia smoothed her ash specked skirt, rubbing the ash deeper into the velvet pile. "Vanarre really can't afford to have its silver trade closed. Your hijacking of the Waylin Mountains, and particularly, of Port Argen, is causing Dad's hair to fall out."

"Tsk," mocked the dragon.

"Of course, no one is starving--and I am grateful that you haven't eaten anyone--but we are all missing the silver trade. Without it we don't have the money to buy other goods, import goods, important things like coffee."

"Ah." Now the dragon understood. "Am I talking with a caffeine fiend?"

"Yes," said Julia grumpily.

"And without the money brought in by the silver trade, the coffee merchants are taking their goods elsewhere."

"Yes." A snarl.

"So, it's not altruism that brings you here, but addiction."

"No! I can live without coffee, if I have to, but the loss of the silver trade has thrown thousands of people out of work-- miners, traders, silversmiths--and that's flowed on to depress other sectors of the economy."

"You sound like a political adviser," said the dragon. He didn't sound pleased.

"Well," conceded Julia. "That is what Dad's royal advisers are saying, but it is commonsense. Vanarre has always been a happy country and we can't just sit around and let you ruin it."

The Southern Dragon huffed, sending the heap of white ash spiraling into the air. "Don't ever join the Diplomatic Corps. I don't think Vanarre can cope with a dragon and a war. Cut the cackle and tell me your proposition."

"Well, the way I see it, you're not guarding the Waylin Mountains because you need silver--everyone knows it's gold dragons love--so you must be hijacking our silver trade so that we have to ransom it from you. The question then is what do we have that a dragon could want. It can't be gold since it's untarnishing silver that Vanarre is famous for. Clearly you don't eat people or livestock."

"I make do with fishing," interjected the dragon. "A giant squid is a splendid meal; tentacles like spaghetti."

Julia shuddered at the thought, but ploughed onward. "So, that leaves only a princess."

"A princess," repeated the dragon thoughtfully. "You?"

"Well, I'm not letting you have my sisters."

"Isn't family loyalty wonderful?" the dragon asked the world at large. "Just out of interest, why would I want a princess?"

"I did wonder about that," admitted Julia. "But it is traditional."

"Tradition is important," said the dragon solemnly.

"And a princess could keep your cave tidy, your scales polished, even cook your giant squid."

"So could a general servant, and probably better."

It was inarguable, so Julia abandoned the point. "Shifting from the general to the particular."

"Why don't we?" agreed the dragon with a lurking amusement that enraged Julia.

Her voice sharpened. "I speak three languages, which you may find useful."

"I speak four. Five including Dracaonic."

"I sing and play the lute."

The dragon shuddered. "Next you'll tell me you're a mime artist, too."

"Certainly not." But Julia was fair. She relented. "Well, not everyone enjoys the lute."

"Really?"

She ignored the provocation. "And then there's my talent."

"Oh, yes?"

"I paint," she said defiantly.

"I can hire a house--ahem--cave painter."

Julia stood and stamped her foot. The powdery ash swirled up. She sneezed.

"Gesundheit," said the dragon.

"Bah," said Julia. She sneezed again. "I paint pictures, and I'm good. So good that sometimes people think my paintings are real."

The dragon yawned.

"Well, then," said Julia. "Why are you holding the silver trade to ransom? What do you want?"

"I thought you'd never ask," said the dragon.

Julia folded her arms and waited.

The Southern Dragon sighed. "I need a princess."

"Duh. What did I just say?"

The dragon held up a talon. "I need a princess to marry me."

Julia sat back down, bruising her bottom on the rock. "Marriage?" She considered the proposal in horrified consternation. "You have noticed that we're different species?"

"You're talking about sex," said the dragon.

"I'm talking common sense. Why do you want a princess bride, anyhow?"

The dragon coughed, and for the first time, looked embarrassed. He shuffled his huge feet. "It's my mom," he rumbled.

"Pardon?" She hadn't quite caught the words.

"It's my mom, all right," roared the dragon. "She wants to see me married."

"Oh." Julia covered her mouth with one hand, but she was too slow. A giggle slipped out.

"That's right, laugh," grumbled the Southern Dragon. "But if I don't get married, Mom will force me to marry Exmeralda, my third cousin four times removed, and Exme's talons are always dirty."

"Couldn't you find a different dragon--dragoness?" asked Julia, smothering her giggles. "One with clean talons."

The dragon gave her a nasty look. "May I remind you that you want my help."

"Yes, yes," said Julia, waving a dismissive hand. "A dragoness?"

"Don't want one," mumbled the dragon.

"Are you gay?"

"No!"

"Keep your scales on," said Julia. She frowned. "Wouldn't your mom object to a princess bride?"

"She couldn't," said the dragon, exhibiting the triumph of a son who thinks he's putting one over his mom. "Some of the most famous dragons have had princess brides."

"I've never heard of any."

"You're not a dragon."

"Fine," said Julia at this piece of rudeness. She kicked at the ground.

"Well?" said the dragon. "Will you marry me and save the kingdom?"

Julia scowled. "I don't even know where you live--I mean, when you're not holding our silver trade to ransom."

"You'll have to take me on trust," said the Southern Dragon.

Julia rolled her eyes. "Great idea."

"Come on, Julia," coaxed the Southern Dragon in a rumbling roar. "For your family, for your kingdom, will you marry me?"

She paused. "Oh, all right."

The wedding was a quiet affair; that is to say, an elopement.

"Dad might be dopey," said Julia. "But he'd lock me in a dungeon rather than let me marry a dragon."

"There's no need to be rude," said the dragon.

Julia gave him a scornful look. Since there was no time like the present, they sought out the Hermit of Holy Wood who was also a priest, and therefore, capable of marrying them.

Although whether he would or not, Julia wasn't willing to wager.

"And you're not to threaten the Hermit," she told the dragon.

"Me?" The dragon sounded scandalised.

"Huh," snorted Julia. "And I can't keep calling you dragon. What's your name?"

"Lucas."

She stopped walking to stare at the dragon. "That doesn't sound very draconic."

"Only to ignorant ears," said Lucas. "Didn't you do any research before marching up here?"

Since she hadn't, Julia huffed again, and started walking. "A velvet dress isn't the right thing to wear to a wedding, and certainly not one covered in ash."

"The Hermit won't mind."

Her long suffering sigh said, "Men, what would they know?"

The path down the mountain circled to right, then the left and stopped abruptly at the Hermit's hut.

"Hallo the house," shouted the dragon.

"Is that anyway to treat a holy man?" scolded Julia. She raised her hand to knock, when the door opened.

"Lucas!" the Hermit sounded delighted. He brushed breadcrumbs off his white beard. "And a lady. Don't tell me you've done it, Lucas? You've found a bride?"

"A princess bride," Lucas confirmed. "Princess Julia, in fact. Julia, close your mouth."

She closed it with a snap. How did the Southern Dragon, scourge of the mountains, know the Hermit? She made a mental vow to find out, later.

"Will you marry us?" Lucas asked the Hermit.

"Delighted. Delighted," said the Hermit. "No church, but then, Lucas, I doubt you'd fit in anything less than a cathedral. Are you ready, my dear?" he asked Julia.

She nodded, thinking of Lucas in one of the fashionable city cathedrals. The noble ladies would faint. So would the archbishop.

"Very good," said the Hermit. And that was that. Within ten minutes, Julia found herself married to Lucas the Southern Dragon. "And I hope you'll be very happy," said the Hermit.

"I hope so, too," said Julia doubtfully, but quite unable to snub the kindly old man.

He waved to them as they departed.

"I'll have to tell my parents," said Julia as they climbed back up the mountain to Lucas's cave.

"Of your sacrifice for the good of the kingdom?" inquired Lucas.

"That I'm safe, but married, and that Dad can stop worrying about you," snapped Julia. She frowned. "I don't think Mum'll like being a dragon's mother in law."

"I can be charming," said Lucas in mock hurt tones. He smiled, evilly. "Besides, think of your own mother in law."

"Oh, goodness." Julia stumbled, and a talon caught and held her elbow. She gave an uncertain giggle. "A lot of people say their mother in law's a dragon, but mine really is."

"I certainly am." A dark shadow drifted over them and a deep voice boomed.

"Mom." Lucas sounded resigned, but not particularly worried. "We'll meet you at my lair."

"I hope you cleaned it for your bride. The last time I saw your treasure heap..."

"He didn't know I was coming," said Julia, vaguely moved to defend her husband although she shook her arm free of his talon. After all, she could hardly claim great tidiness herself. She brushed once more at her ash-ruined skirt. She thought about her last statement. "We didn't know you were coming. We could have delayed the wedding."

"A nice thought," said Julia's mother-in-law. "But if I'd been fifteen minutes earlier, there'd have been no wedding."

"Why?"

"Can't this wait till we're at the lair?" suggested Lucas.

"No," said his womenfolk.

"Fine," he stepped to the side of the path, bringing Julia with him, and giving his mom room to land.

She did so in a gentle swirl of dust that coated her opalescent, blush pink scales and set Julia coughing.

"My name is Maura," said the dragoness grandly.

Coughing, Julia flapped her hand in a pleased-to-meet-you gesture.

Lucas sighed. Smoke issued from his nostrils, adding to Julia's breathing problems. "Mom, this is Julia, Princess of Vanarre. Julia, this is Mom."

"You know, Lucas, if you don't want her to asphyxiate, you might want to stop smouldering at me. Besides, sulking is so unattractive."

Julia nodded vigorous agreement.

"I am not sulking." Lucas inhaled and held his breath for a count of twenty. When he exhaled, the smoke had gone. "Why would I sulk? I won."

"Leaving me to explain the situation to Exmeralda's parents, and the girl, herself."

"That seems fair to me," said Lucas with silky politeness. "After all, you're the one who brought up the idea of an arranged marriage."

"For your own good."

Julia held a hand to her chest as her breathing steadied. "Why would an arranged marriage help Lucas?"

"It would settle him down. He needs responsibility. At the moment, he's too airy fairy. He meddles."

"Like with Vanarre's silver trade," said Julia, feeling suddenly in sympathy with Maura.

The dragoness inclined her head in graceful agreement. "Lucas's trouble is he doesn't consider the consequences of his actions."

"I do, too." Lucas stopped, then cleared his throat with a bass rumble.

Julia grinned. Family dynamics, you had to love them. And it seemed even dragons could be trapped into juvenile patterns. Do too/do not.

"Marrying Exmeralda would have made him responsible for her actions, and Exmeralda has a lot of problems."

"Bad tempered, brainless and dirty," said Lucas.

"She's not that bad." Maura jerked back, shocked by his words. "She had a bad upbringing, but I'd not marry you to a harridan. I believe she can be saved."

"Mom, she ate a knight last month."

Julia shivered, and pressed against Lucas. She appreciated his outrage.

He shifted so she rested in the crook of his elbow.

"I hadn't heard." Maura sounded thoughtful with second thoughts. "Was it a clean kill?"

"No."

"That's bad." Maura shivered her wings in the manner of a human shrugging off nastiness. "Still, you could have told me. There was no need to marry a princess."

"It puts an end to your matchmaking attempts."

"Yes, but...Lucas, I know I taught you what happens to dragons who marry princesses."

Julia gripped one of Lucas's talons and held it tightly. "What? What happens to dragons who marry princesses?"

"They become heroes."

Julia sniffed, offended. She released Lucas's talon. "We princesses aren't so bad. I call that rude."

Crr-crr-crr. Mother and son laughed.

"Daft," said Lucas as he hiccoughed a final laugh. "The hero badge isn't for wedding a princess--although with you, I'm sure I'll earn it. The hero tag is because our marriage is a sign I'm willing to interest myself in human affairs. That means magical and practical challenges of hero status."

"Oh. So that's why the hermit approved of our marriage."

"And that's why I wanted to stop your marriage." Maura brought her large head close to Julia. "I'm sure you're a nice child, but I want to keep my child safe. I don't want him hurt defending your kingdom."

"I understand," said Julia. "But, oh dear, this is funny." She laughed so hard she slid from Lucas's elbow and sat on the ground.

The two dragons stared at her, baffled.

"You see." Julia made an heroic effort to control her laughter. "The biggest threat to Vanarre isn't magical or dangerous or...or...anything. It's my family. Dad needs an adviser. My brother needs finding. My mom needs a friend. And my sisters need spanking. Just yesterday they tried to capture a griffin. We're chaos."

She sent a sparkling look in Maura's direction. "You want Lucas to have responsibility. If he takes on my family, he'll have it in spades."

"Interesting." Maura's eyes narrowed in concentration. "And it does shine a different light on things."

"I thought I'd fight sea monsters," said Lucas. "I've been practising with the giant squid."

Julia shuddered. "We have a navy," she said firmly.

"And you, my boy, have responsibilities," boomed his mom. Lucas sighed, but this time, without smoking. "Oh, very well. If you'll climb aboard, Julia, we'll fly down to the palace. I suppose I should meet my new responsibilities."

"Very good," said Maura. "I'll come with you. If the Queen needs a friend, I think I fit the picture. After all, I have experience with troublesome children." She extended her large wings and flipped into the air.

"Lucas." Julia walked around till she could frown at him face to face. Sapphire eyes gleamed back at her. "You did this on purpose. You've set us all up."

"Yes." He grinned, showing large teeth. "Your father will find me an excellent strategist. Last winter, I was getting bored with life, and then I saw you berating an ogre and sending it away, club dragging. I knew you were the woman for me."

"Because I shout loudly?"

"Because you have courage. And Julia, about consummating our marriage."

"Hmm?" she answered warily. New dragon husbands seemed full of surprises. She'd have to stay on her toes.

"I'm a shapeshifter. Want a ride?"

Mud Puddles, A Dragon And A Giraffe

Jeremiah's feet landed in the middle of the murky waters of his Mississippi mud hole. Splash-splash and 'slop—slop, slurp,' went the water and mud as it lapped over his white sneakers. His mom's voice echoed briefly, "Don't get those new sneakers dirty, or I'll hit the roof Jeremiah." He scooted his feet to the left, then to the right, getting the most splatter effect possible from twisting his sneakers. It sure was fun outside after a rain; there were mud puddles, crawly worms, and even the air smelled wet. Mississippi must be the best place to live in the whole world!

Jeremiah smiled and looked down at his sneakers; Mom's voice was more clear, "Don't get those new sneakers dirty, or I'll hit the roof Jeremiah." Cold sweat beaded across Jeremiah's forehead and the back of his neck prickled with guilt. His stomach leaped up his throat and tried to jump from his mouth. He clasped his hand over his lips just in time. Mom said she 'would hit the roof' if he ruined another pair of shoes. Mom never broke a promise; and he was afraid if she saw his shoes, she would hurt herself when she 'hit the roof'. It was up to him to keep his mom from being hurt.

Jeremiah was eight, but he recalled Mr. Ben his second-grand teacher saying that he was a smart intellect. Think— he had to come up with a plan. The answer came as easy as slipping a brownie from Aunt Kim's bakery when she wasn't looking. He knew what to do.

He scampered to the rear of the house and sat down on the steps leading to the garden. He tugged off his shoes, wiped the mud from them onto his face and shirt, and then tousled his hair for 'effect'. He threw his shoes in the garden's compost pile and dashed back to the front of the house. Sadie, his golden retriever, thought he was playing with her as he passed; but he ignored her.

"Mom, oh mom...help please...," he wailed loudly.

Jeremiah's mom came to the front door, "Jeremiah, what's wrong, where are you?" She pushed the door open looking toward the front yard.

He stumbled in front of her, moaning, and collapsed to the ground, "Mommy...I'm here," he said more faint this time.

"For gracious sakes, what has happened to you and where are your shoes?"

"It was awful, Mommeeeee, just awful.

A great big dragon jumped out from behind the tree and landed on me. I swear I didn't do a thing to him; he just came at me. He tried to eat me, but I kicked and kicked so the only part he ate was my sneakers. Oh, Mommy, I'm so sorry he ate my new shoes!"

Mom looked a bit puzzled said, "If a dragon ate your shoes, where is he?"

Jeremiah knew what his Mom was trying to do, but he was still in control, "After the dragon ate my shoes, he laid down across the sidewalk. Then, this great big giraffe came running clumsily down the same sidewalk, scooped up the dragon and swallowed him whole.

What could I do? There's no way I was putting my hand down a giraffe's throat, my arms are too short!"

Sadie darted to the front porch and then circled Jeremiah. She dropped something at his feet then tackled him to the ground. Mom reached down and picked up Sadie's gift of a white sneaker covered in mud and compost.

"Well, what do you know?" Mom said, handing the sneaker to him.

"Well, Mom....Sadie is a 'real' retriever I suppose. She braved the dragon and giraffe to 'retrieve' my shoes," he said pursing his lips and wrinkling his nose. Sadie was too good a retriever.

The Butterfly And The Fire Breathing Dragon

A long, yes very long time ago there was a dragon, a most evil, wicked and feared fire breathing Dragon called Dre. Or so it was believed that he was most evil and wicked – but later, and as the story will tell, it will be learned that Dre had been shunned by most which is why he turned bitter, evil and wicked. Until one special day, one very special day he'd meet and cross paths with a butterfly, a butterfly named Faith.

Faith lived in Butterfly Ville with siblings Hope, and Harmony. Faith lived a most joyous and happy life, fluttering through life with Hope and Harmony until most recently when she'd awaken to learn that her siblings had simply vanished. Thinking perhaps they were just playing an old fashioned game of butterfly hide and seek Faith flew from one corner of the tree to the other, looking from one lily to the other until she could stand it no longer and called out, "come on you two, come out, come out wherever you are!" Surely now they would fly out and laugh at her for not being able to find them but neither Hope nor Harmony appeared. As minutes turned to hours daylight to dark and there was still no sign of Hope and Harmony Faith cried herself to sleep , alone and confused not knowing what tomorrow would hold in store. Exhausted and with no other choice but to sleep Faith drifted off hopeful that with the start of a brand new day perhaps she would awaken to find both Hope and Harmony.

And with the next day's burning rays of sun Faith stretched her wings, yawning to meet the brand new day. Quickly remembering she had a mission today and that mission was to search for Hope and Harmony and search she would! Faith flew from tree to tree, lily to lily once again making sure Hope and Harmony weren't carrying out some silly little game and in despair after not finding either Faith entered into the deep dark forest. Although worry she did as she heard tales about Dre the fire breathing dragon, Faith knew there was, just simply no other choice. So deep and deeper into the forest Faith flew. Along the way Faith ran into Rattle, hissing and snarling he spoke to her and said ssss faith, I ssss seen Hope and I ssss saw Harmony – they were behind the rock wall just a few ssss short ssss steps away, Faith hurriedly flew to the rock wall. Hope, Harmony she cried, it's me it's Faith! And just as she had landed on the lily by the rock wall Rattle tried to catch her, ssss swallow her. And just as suddenly as Rattle tried to swallow Faith there was a shrill cry "watch out" ....and Faith flew to the nearest and highest tree limb. "Whew", cried Faith thanks for saving my life. Why who are you? Bunny is my name said the brown long eared rabbit. Dear Faith, what brings you, alone, into the depths of the forest? Sobbing Faith explained she couldn't find her siblings and would search anywhere and everywhere she could until she found them. And then just as Bunny was getting ready to tell her about Dre there was a ROAR so loud and so scary, they both huddled together and scattered into the nearest cove they could find. And when they found the courage to peek out what seemed like hours later, they saw Dre, the fire breathing dragon, with big dark eyes, and green scaley body and why, the longest tail Faith had ever seen, but fire? Faith saw no fire.

Funny, although both Bunny and Faith were trembling with great fear, Faith thought hmm, Dre didn't look evil and wicked and, well, he wasn't breathing fire. Perhaps the tale of Dre and the fire was just that, a tale, after all. But Bunny begged Faith not to leave the cove where it was safe – and in that moment Faith stood tall and explained she was on a mission and had to find Hope and Harmony. Faith appeared at the opening of the cove and startled Dre who wasn't expecting anyone to be in the forest. Suddenly fire emerged from Dre's mouth and Faith had to fly hurriedly to avoid being burned, and in her haste, she hadn't realized she didn't fly quite far enough away from Dre. Faith fell to the ground a wing singed unable to fly any further any longer. Bunny watched in horror but, frozen with fear, couldn't find the courage to come out of hiding and help her. Surely Dre would not them being in his forest, surely Dre would.....and then Bunny, when he couldn't imagine any longer saw something that he never in a million years would have ever imagined he'd see....it was Dre and, did he see a small tear in the fire breathing dragon's eyes, he wondered? And as he watched he saw that Dre was headed to a small stream where he'd placed some water in his mouth, carried it back and let it flow gently over Faith's singed wing. Shaken from the cold water and the fear of waking up to seeing Dre directly above her Faith tried to fly away again falling to the ground.

And it was then that Dre spoke, I didn't mean to harm you I am not evil and wicked I am alone and confused. And Faith came to realize that Dre was very much like herself. Faith tried to perch herself along the rock wall resting to try and get her strength back and she explained to Dre that it was the loss of her siblings Hope and Harmony that brought her into the deep woods where normally she wouldn't enter, she knew this was his territory but simply, she just had to find them no matter what the risk. And Dre putting his dragon hand out for her to fly into explained that it was also unlike him to venture out of the deep woods where he'd been outcast to for many, many years. And as Faith and Dre shared their tears and their laughter Dre explained to Faith that all he really wanted was to be liked and to have friends. And just as Faith and Dre discovered they shared many things Bunny appeared, Rattle appeared, and creatures unknown to them all appeared. And in the distance fluttering and flying back to Faith were Hope and Harmony, and it was at that very moment there was a peace and serenity in the deep woods unlike any had ever known or seen before. Among an understanding of creatures great and small – there was Faith, there was Hope and there was Harmony.

Dinosaurs In My Bed

Andrew lay shivering in his bed. The sky was alive with booming sounds and brilliant flashes just outside his window.

Fifteen minutes ago he asked, "Mom, will the storm last long?"

"Please, don't worry," she said. "The weatherman promised it would pass over Truro quickly. Now get some sleep."

Except it didn't; and he couldn't.

Andrew listened to his alarm clock. "Tick...Tick...Tock." The night seemed to go on forever. Seconds turned into minutes.

Then into what seemed like hours.

Above the house, loud lightning crashes made him duck further under the blankets. Outside thunder even rattled his window.

Should he go into his parent's room? But then he was a big boy now. And he had to be brave. Dad even helped him prepare for this bad weather.

Just in case it lasted all night.

Now his backpack was hidden under the blankets. It was filled with favorite toys, games and comic books. Even "Panda" bear he had since the age of two.

Mom made sure Andrew also had a few goodies. A huge bag of popcorn was close to his right side. And a bag of rippled chips was on the other.

His family had gone tenting in Cape Breton, last weekend. So he was now a boy with camping experience. And he knew how to be brave.

What was moving around his toes? "Ouch, that hurt," his trembling voice, whispered. The noise outside was so loud Andrew could hardly think.

Through the window, a dark sky blocked out the stars.

The boy was suddenly nervous. What was under the blanket? He was curious and rummaged through his backpack.

"OMIGOSH," Andrew said. "I forgot my flashlight."

He slid out of bed and hurled himself across the floor. Andrew hunted around until he found it in the top dresser drawer.

Quickly jumping back into bed, he forced cold feet down to the very end. Bare toes rested on something rough and sharp. Now it seemed to be crawling around his ankles.

Yikes! He wasn't alone in bed!

He checked under the covers where it was black as coal, almost like being outside. Instead of gleaming stars lit up, spots looked more like eyes.

Roaring came from behind his left leg.

Andrew chewed on his left thumb and turned on the flashlight. "That terrifying sound couldn't be...?" he hesitated.

Yes, a dinosaur! But that was impossible, wasn't it? Dinosaurs couldn't fit under bed covers belonging to a little boy, living inside his house. Right?

Wrong. Staring back at him was a Stegosaurus. And it tasted his Hostess vinegar chips, the one small bag with a few morsels left.

"Get away, you!" Andrew bellowed, trying to be brave. The animal rumbled something back under the blanket-sky and hurried into a shadowy corner.

New noises caught the boy's attention. His flashlight helped pick out moving shadows. What was going on? he wondered. There was a Triceratops and a Deinonychus. And a Tyranosaurus!

"Run!" Andrew yelled. Suddenly he felt like he was the only one alive on the planet. But he was still under his blanket that seemed to expand in the distance and even high above him.

He searched for somewhere to hide.

Cold feet could barely move. It was like a different world under the blankets. His heart marched to the beat of a drum. Lightning zipped then zapped under his blanket-sky. Large animals began to chase smaller ones.

Racing toward him was a Dicraeosaurus. This was a peaceful plant eater and would not hurt him. But, Andrew couldn't take any chances.

He pulled a fire engine from his backpack. Jumping into the front seat, Andrew turned the siren on full velocity. All it did was hurt his ears.

A Ceratosaurus and Albertosaurus bounded after him. They were like large friendly dogs wanting to play. But Andrew didn't wish to get crushed.

He stepped on the gas pedal. And the fire engine leaped forward.

Soon, the road became a narrow path, aiming straight for the forest. Andrew quickly parked. Then he laced on new sneakers from his backpack.

He also brought his whistle. Shrill blowing warned everything to get out of his way. A flurry of feet escaped down the trail, each step pounding hard.

One arm held tightly to 'Panda.'

The wind blew off his cap sending it into the distance. Branches snatched at his face. He didn't want to get squashed or eaten by those dinosaurs.

The storm outside was nothing compared to wild animals chasing him under his blanket. How did all of this happen anyhow?

Growls and speeding feet kept pace behind him. Reaching into his backpack Andrew grabbed his roller blades. Now, he thought, it should be easy to skate away safely.

That is, until a sneaky tree root sent him headfirst into the mud.

Now it was hurry-up time to climb a tree.

"Mom, where are you?" Andrew shouted. "Daddd!" Skinny legs scrambled up the trunk. And like a monkey climbed higher from branch to branch.

Suddenly between two limbs was the head of a Brontosaurus. It smiled as it chewed a mouthful of leaves. "What's your problem?" it seemed to say.

"Andrew! ANDREWWW!" someone called. Voices seemed to move back and forth and around like echoes. Yes, people were shouting his name!

The boy hastily threw off his blankets, sat up, and stared at mom and dad. He blinked as morning's sun peeked between Venetian blinds.

"Panda" was still tucked securely under his arm.

"I see you found our surprises under your blankets," mom said.

Andrew looked blankly at his mom.

"You know. Remember the dinosaur models you asked for last week?"

"And I'm proud of you," dad said. "Look how neatly you stacked them on your dresser."

Andrew felt weird as dad pointed.

In a neat row was a parade of colorful dinosaurs. They were following a friendly Dicraeosaurus, with a ferocious looking Tyrannosaurus Rex at the end of the line.

Leading the whole group was a figure of a little boy.

And he was holding tightly to a teddy bear.

Crutches The Triceratops

Once upon a time, there was dinosaur named crutch who had really long horns, even longer than his fathers and his mothers' but, crutch hated his very longhorns. "I don't think my horns are longer than yours," he told his friend stretch one day but his horns were even bigger and longer than stretch's horns. "I bet trex would help me get rid of my Longhorns," said crutch hopeful "I don't think that's a good idea," said stretch but, crutch did not listen and went to find trex.

Crutch went out to look for trex and when he found him he told trex how much he hated his longhorns so trex told him "let me eat your head and you won't have to worry about your horns anymore" crutch thought for a moment "and it won't even hurt" said Trex. "No thank you trex, if you take my head then I can't have thoughts and ideas and I won't be able to eat anymore" but trex did not listen to crutch and opened his mouth to eat crutches head, however, crutch did not let him and used his longhorn to push trex away and ran as fast as he could and crutch began realised how important his horns where and he began to love his very longhorns and never wanted to be rid of them again.

The Dragons Of China

Before China had people, they had Dragons! There were hundreds of different dragons who would soon play a very important role to the Chinese culture. But of these dragons was one who was very important, as through his wisdom he created the idea of forming the land that the people of China now live on.

These dragons were sick of flying around and having nothing to do and having no purpose. It was not until the oldest and most wisest dragon thought, that maybe they could make a place where animals could live and serve them, and in return worship the dragons. That way they would have a purpose in life and wouldn't be left to continue flying oblivious to anything around them.

So, the wisest dragon called a meeting for all dragons. He told them that they wanted to make land and animals who would worship them. All of the dragons raised their heads high and all agreed.

Very quickly, each dragon chose what they wanted to make or bring to this new land. A large red dragon brought festiveness and happiness to this land, so that all could come together and celebrate dragons while having fun.

A small green dragon with dark green spikes said that he would create trees and plants.

A long and very thin white dragon created Air, and a blue fat dragon made water. Soon many things were made, like the sky, stars, sun and moon, food, light and joy, the list continued. But there was one thing missing. The animals that would worship them and they could serve.

The wisest Dragon, who thought of the idea was told to create these beings, so first he made a very large and heavy creature that was black and white and would only eat plants. He had made the Panda. Soon followed he made a bird who was also black and white called the Crane.

Soon and very quickly he created many animals and with more colors but now was time for his most finest creation, The Human! These were the animals that would help look after their creations and who would worship them.

Thinking long and hard, he visualized how they would look. They would have long arms and legs, only two of each. They would have hands with fingers and thumbs so they could lift, carry, create and look after everything around them. Soon the dragon made a body followed by a head with eyes to see, ears to hear, mouth to speak and eat a nose to smell. He made both a female and a male so they could continue their race. At last, China was made, the dragons were all worshiped and life was beautiful.

Witches, Dinosaurs And A Princess

Once upon a time, there was a witch and it was a terrible witch and there was also a Princess. The witch tried to attack, but the Princess got out of the way. Then the witch's friends came to help the witch, but luckily, the Princess had a time machine.

So she went back in time to see the dinosaurs and she had lots of adventures, like when the dinosaur took off his nose and threw it in the pond and they had to swim to find it. Even though the Princess was having fun, she wanted to go home. It was then she realised that a dinosaur had eaten the time machine, but this did not matter because the Princess knew if she waited a few million years, she would eventually get back home.

The Earthwyrm

Annie was the gardener's daughter, and she was in trouble. Her father was not just any gardener: he was the Royal Gardener. Day after day he tended the palace gardens, mowing and hoeing, seeding and weeding. When she wasn't at school Annie followed him around with the wheelbarrow. She was supposed to be learning the trade.

"This will be your job one day," her father told her. "It runs in our family, being Royal Gardener."

Annie just smiled and turned a cartwheel. She didn't say anything because she didn't want to disappoint her father; but she would much rather play in the garden than work there.

The beech avenues were perfect for hide and seek. She could climb the apple trees in the orchard, roll down the grassy knoll from the sundial on the top, or pretend she was lost in the Maze.

Best of all, she liked to lie on her stomach on the palace lawn, watching the tiny garden creatures battle through their miniature jungle. She hunted spiders and followed ant-trails and observed the bees, all the time with the comfortable click-click of her father's shears in the background.

Then one day, the shears stopped.

"Ow!" said her father. "Ouch!" He clutched at his back.

"You'd better go and lie down," said Annie.

"Lie down? I've got far too much to do! I've got to get everything ready for King Florizel's Garden Party tomorrow." He tried to straighten up, and winced. "Ooh, that's painful!"

"Don't worry," said Annie. "Go home. I'll do the garden for you." She took him firmly by the arm and led him back to their house.

Her father tried to protest, but not very hard. His back was hurting too much.

"Don't forget the shrubs- "

"I'll prune them."

"And the lawn- "

"I'll mow it."

"And the maze- "

"I'll weed it."

"It all has to be perfect for tomorrow!" he called anxiously as Annie left.

"It will be!" she answered blithely.

Back in the palace gardens, she climbed to the top of the grassy hill and stood by the sundial, leaning on her father's spade. She was in charge now.

From here she could see the whole garden. And now that she took a good look, there was far more to do than she had supposed.

The lawn really was shaggy. The shrubbery needed a good haircut too. The brick paths of the maze were blotched with weeds, the nursery beds were overgrown, and all the glass panes in the greenhouses were broken.

She turned to look over the high wall into the kitchen garden. It was full of birds busily stripping the blackcurrant bushes bare.

Quickly she switched her gaze to the rose garden: the King's pride and glory. Today the air above it shimmered - but not with heat. A haze of greenfly swarmed around the roses.

Annie groaned almost as loudly as her father had. Now she understood why he always said there was too much work here for one man.

"Why did I tell him I could do all this?" she cried. "Where do I begin?"

Angrily, she plunged her father's spade into the ground.

"There's far too much! I'll never get it done!"

Then she sat down rather suddenly, because the ground had moved.

A ripple ran through the hill like a small earthquake. Annie sat on top of it with her mouth open and her eyes popping. She stared at the gash that her spade had cut in the grass.

It was slowly widening. The sundial tilted and fell over. Longer and longer grew the crack, spreading like black lightning, until it ran all the way round the hill.

"Just like a boiled egg about to be opened," thought Annie. "And I'm sitting right on the top!"

She threw herself across the crack and rolled down the slope.

She was only just in time. The crack was still spiralling its way down like an apple unpeeling itself. And then the top started to lift off.

The whole hill shuddered. The grassy peel was tossed away into the air. Clods of turf whizzed over Annie's head and thudded softly on the lawn behind her.

She stared at the unpeeled hill. It was made of neither soil nor rock, but something else: something coiled, green and wetly glistening.

A long, thin neck uncurled. It looked like a snake - but it was far, far bigger than the grass snakes that sometimes dozed around the sundial.

The head turned a sleepy yellow gaze on Annie, stretched out towards her and yawned in her face. It had a great many teeth which looked extremely sharp.

Shutting its mouth with a snap, it opened its golden eyes very wide.

"Well?" it said with a hiss. "What did you wake me up for?"

"P-pardon?" stammered Annie.

"Slugs in the cabbages? Locusts in the greenhouse? Or just an invading army of ants?"

"None of those," said Annie, quite bewildered. "I didn't mean to wake you up at all. Who are you?"

The yellow eyes gleamed at her balefully.

"Who am I?" it hissed. "Don't you know? I thought everyone knew me. Why, King Florizel the Fourth even gave me the freedom of the city!"

"Did he?"

"Certainly! For I," announced the creature with great dignity, "am the Earthwyrm."

"You don't look like an earthworm," said Annie.

"Not a worm. A wyrm. With a y. Otherwise known as a wyvern. Oh, all right then, a dragon, but of a most superior sort. I suppose you have heard of dragons?"

"Oh, yes. But where are your wings?"

The Earthwyrm uncoiled itself a little more. A single pair of legs appeared. Annie waited for the other pair, but that seemed to be all there were. With a creaking sound, two rather damp and crumpled wings unfolded and waved feebly.

"Ouch," said the Earthwyrm. "My back! I've been curled up for too long."

"My Dad gets backache," said Annie sympathetically. "He's the Royal Gardener, but he can't work because of his back, so I've got to do it. Oh, dear! And now look at the state of that hill, on top of everything else!"

"He's what?" roared the Earthwyrm.

"Who's what?"

"Your father! Royal Gardener? A human?" It spouted an angry blast of orange sparks. Annie took a few steps backwards.

"Why not?" she said stoutly. "So was his father, and his grandmother. It's in the family."

"Disgraceful! I'm the Royal Gardener! An Earthwyrm has always been in charge. Why couldn't King Florizel have waited for me to wake up?" It blew out another cloud of sparks with an affronted WHOOF.

Annie wondered how to put it tactfully. "Maybe because King Florizel the Fourth isn't around any more," she said. "He hasn't been around for three hundred years. We're onto King Florizel the Fourteenth now."

The golden eyes dulled. "Ah," said the Earthwyrm. "Hmmm." It stared around the garden.

"I must have overslept," it said regretfully at last. "That's the trouble with hibernating. Never know when you're going to wake up. I can see now that things have changed considerably. And not for the better!"

"My father does his best," said Annie. "But there's an awful lot of garden, and there's only him and me to do it. And tomorrow it's the Royal Garden Party. I'll never manage it all!" Despair overcame her.

"I should think not. A human, indeed! What this garden needs is an Earthwyrm."

Annie was nettled. "I suppose you think you could do it in no time!"

"Certainly," it answered haughtily. "However, I'm not going to. It's not my job any more."

Annie took a deep breath. If the garden wasn't ready, her father would be in disgrace. She swallowed her pride and said humbly,

"I wish you would show me how it could be done."

The wyrm half-closed its eyes. "Like I said, I'm not the Royal Gardener now."

"But you could be again," suggested Annie, "after my father, if you don't mind waiting twenty years till he retires."

The eyes snapped open. "Twenty years? That's nothing," said the Earthwyrm. "Could it be arranged?"

"Oh, yes," said Annie earnestly, giving away her inheritance without a sigh. "But only if the garden is ready by tomorrow!"

"What time is it?"

"Two o'clock."

"Hmm." The Earthwyrm unfurled its claws, stretching like a cat. "Let's see. It really has been dreadfully neglected. It's a challenge all right! I shall start with the lawn."

"The lawnmower's in the shed."

"Lawnmower? Modern nonsense!" said the Earthwyrm scornfully. And with a loud clap of its wings it rose straight up into the air, unrolling the last of its long, long tail.

It was a very thin tail, Annie noticed: as thin and flat as a knife. The end of it was barbed like an arrowhead.

"Watch this!" The Earthwyrm hovered for an instant high above her, then turned and swooped towards the lawn. It gathered speed so fast that Annie was convinced it was going to crash right into her.

She dived into the shrubbery. Behind her came a rush of air as the Earthwyrm skimmed the lawn. Gliding fast and low, it began to sweep its tail from side to side.

It was raining grass. The wyrm swooped to and fro, scything with its tail until the entire lawn was shaved in a rather unusual fantail pattern.

"Pretty," said Annie, shaking grass cuttings from her hair. "What about the bushes?"

"Easy," said the dragon tersely. It landed by the shrubbery and whipped its tail back and forth, slashing at the leaves.

Annie ran to gather up the clippings, ducking to avoid the tail whenever it swished past her. Soon her wheelbarrow was overflowing.

"The maze is full of weeds," she began; but the Earthwyrm was already on its way. It moved with something between a crawl and a slither, dragging itself on its two scaly legs.

At the entrance to the maze, it lowered its head and breathed long, red tongues of flame across the paving. The weeds turned black and shrivelled up. The wyrm crawled further into the maze and disappeared around the corner.

"Hallo?" called Annie after several minutes. "Are you lost?"

The Earthwyrm reappeared. "The very idea! I planted this maze."

"It's a very good one," Annie said politely.

"Mazes are my speciality. And that avenue of beeches: that was mine. And the kitchen garden..." It broke off and cocked its head, eyes glinting. "Birds? What are they doing there?"

It rapidly slithered to the high wall round the kitchen garden. It sprang to the top, wings arched high above its head, its tail swishing furiously. Opening its jaws wide, it roared.

Dozens of startled birds shot up from the blackcurrant bushes, screeching with terror, and flapped away as fast as they could.

"Good riddance," grunted the Earthwyrm. "They won't be back for a while." Reaching down to take a mouthful of blackcurrants, it chomped them thoughtfully. Purple juice trickled down its neck.

"How are you with greenfly?" asked Annie. "The roses are covered with them."

"Greenfly don't scare so easily. Different tactics are needed."

The Earthwyrm crawled swiftly to the rose garden. Rearing up, it cleared its throat with a sound like sand being shovelled.

"WHOO!" It huffed a cloud of dense black smoke that wafted gently across the flowers.

Annie coughed and choked. Her eyes were watering. As the smoke drifted away, she saw thousands of tiny green bodies tumbling from the roses and hitting the ground.

"Harumph," rasped the Earthwyrm. "Excuse me. Now, what's next?"

"The orchard? The apples are starting to fall, and the King won't want them squishing underfoot."

"I'm not a fruit-picker," said the dragon haughtily. "That's servants' work. But I'll give you a lift."

So with a basket over each arm, Annie hoisted herself gingerly onto the Earthwyrm's back. Its skin was cool and slightly damp. When it sprang into the air, there was nothing to hang on to but the slippery edges of its wings.

She did not enjoy the apple-picking. The Earthwyrm kept moving just as she was reaching for the furthest apples, and she decided that it was doing it on purpose. But at last there were several baskets full of apples lined up on the grass.

"I think that's everything," the Earthwyrm said, and yawned. "Dear me, two hours to spare till sun-down."

"It's not everything!" cried Annie. "What about that hill you unpeeled? Look at it! It's in a worse state than the rest of the garden put together!"

"Oops," said the Earthwyrm. It slithered back across the neatly shaven lawn towards the bare, black mound. After crawling twice around the hill, it lay staring up at it, tail twitching.

"Problem," it muttered.

Annie began to pick up the ragged shreds of turf and stack them in her wheelbarrow. "It's no good trying to patch it up with these!" she said severely. "I'll have to put them on the compost heap."

"Bring back some glass."

"What?"

"Glass! From the greenhouses. Hurry up! What are you waiting for?"

Annie shook her head. "Crazy," she muttered. All the same, she fetched a barrow-load of broken glass and tipped it in a crashing heap by the Earthwyrm's tail.

"Now go and get some more," it ordered. "Lots more. And bring those overgrown seedlings from the nursery beds."

Annie opened her mouth to protest, but the wyrm had turned its back on her to nose through the shattered glass. She sighed, and set off again with the wheel-barrow.

In between barrow-loads she watched the Earthwyrm, trying to puzzle out what it was doing. It had laid glass in jagged paths all around the hill, right the way up to the sundial at the top. The whole thing looked rather untidy and decidedly dangerous.

"Crazy paving," commented Annie under her breath. She didn't think much of it.

The earthwyrm slithered down to where she stood.

"Stand well away!" it warned. Then it sucked in hard, and breathed out a stream of fire.

The flames that licked around the hill started off red, as before. But this time, as the Earthwyrm puffed out more and more, they gradually changed colour to orange, then to yellow, and finally to dazzling white-hot.

Annie had to back away, shielding her eyes. The hill steamed and hissed. Round and round stalked the

Earthwyrm, pausing only now and then to take huge, gasping breaths and breathe out yet more fire.

At last it stopped and lay down, panting. The hill was covered in a cloud of steam. When the fog parted, Annie gasped.

"Oh, my!"

The spiky trails of broken glass were gone. In their place lay a shimmering maze whose myriad paths intertwined in elegant crystal knots.

The glass had melted. It was jagged no longer, but smooth, and full of bubbles. As the sun broke through a cloud, the twisting paths shone like rivers of liquid gold.

"Just the planting up to do," whispered the Earthwyrm hoarsely.

"But you look exhausted!"

It shook its tired head. "You do the top, I'll do the bottom. Watch out for the glass. It's hot."

Together they planted the seedlings between the loops of glass. Annie worked down from sundial, the dragon worked up, and they met in the middle just as the sun was setting.

"If the King doesn't like that, there'll be no pleasing him," said the Earthwyrm gruffly.

"He'll like it," Annie said. "I do." She made a low and sweeping bow. "Thank you, Earthwyrm. Would you like to come home for some supper?"

The Earthwyrm inclined its long neck gracefully. "How kind."

"What do you eat?" asked Annie with some trepidation.

But the wyrm said promptly, "Eggs. Keep the pesky birds down, I say. Think they can fly! Hah!"

So the Earthwyrm came to Annie's house for supper, and stayed for three days. It sat in the garden with Annie's father, drinking ginger beer and smoking. Annie's father smoked a pipe; but the Earthwyrm just smoked. Every now and then it crunched up a raw egg, shell and all.

It got on very well with Annie's father. They talked about pruning and propagating and layering and grafting until Annie grew quite bored.

"I'd be glad if you took over as Royal Gardener," said her father at last. "You don't need to wait for twenty years. I'd like to retire early. The job doesn't suit my back." He turned to Annie. "Would you mind very much, Annie?"

Annie looked up from the grass where she was watching beetles.

"Actually, I never wanted to be Royal Gardener anyway," she admitted. "I'd much rather be Royal Beekeeper instead."

"That's all right then," said her father; and they sat peacefully listening to the sounds of the Garden Party drifting over from the palace. It sounded like a great success.

"Just one thing puzzles me," said Annie's father, pulling on his pipe. "You dragons are supposed to love treasure, aren't you? Don't you all have hoards of gold? Or are Earthwyrms different?"

"Not so different," said the dragon. "Gold is my favourite, too." It gazed around the little garden at the petals glowing in the evening sun: marigolds, nasturtiums, goldenrod, and sunflowers.

"Treasure," said the Earthwyrm softly.

CPSIA information can be obtained
at www.ICGtesting.com
Printed in the USA
BVHW090017240421
605736BV00010B/187